"I want to ma

There, he'd said it.

Kate's head dropped a moment, and then she met his eyes.
The anger was now replaced with a look of sorrow.

"You cannot buy me, Mr. Pickett."

In the past Sam's persistence had served him well. In his
mind, this was no different. He wanted her. It was only left
for them to strike a bargain.

"I need you, Kate. Lady as pretty as you could be a real
help to me wrangling up investors for the railroad. Miners
love a pretty girl. You'd keep their interest while we sell
stock."

"And share your bed."

Sam smiled, letting his grasp soften as he drew his hand
away in a long caress.

He leaned in to whisper in her ear. "We'd be good
together, you and I. I can feel it."

* * *

Sierra Bride
Harlequin® Historical #956—August 2009

Praise for Jenna Kernan's Books

Outlaw Bride
"Kernan creates an engaging and fascinating story."
—*Romantic Times BOOKreviews*

High Plains Bride
"Those who enjoy Westerns or tales of lovers reunited will not want to miss this book. It has found a place on my keeper shelf and I know I will be reading it again."
—*All About Romance*

The Trapper
"Kernan's engaging characters and a colorful backdrop… make this classic western romance something special."
—*Romantic Times BOOKreviews*

Turner's Woman
"Makes for tip-top reading."
—*Romantic Times BOOKreviews*

Winter Woman
"Presents a fascinating portrait of the early days of the West and the extraordinary men and woman who traveled and settled in the area…Kernan has a knack for writing a solid western with likable characters."
—*Romantic Times BOOKreviews*

"*Winter Woman* is an exciting, no holds barred story with unforgettable characters. Ms. Kernan's first novel is a winner!"
—*Rendezvous*

"With this strong debut, Jenna Kernan puts her name on the list of writers to watch for and *Winter Woman* may just be the start of a long career."
—*The Romance Reader*

JENNA KERNAN

Sierra Bride

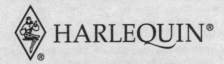

HARLEQUIN®

TORONTO • NEW YORK • LONDON
AMSTERDAM • PARIS • SYDNEY • HAMBURG
STOCKHOLM • ATHENS • TOKYO • MILAN • MADRID
PRAGUE • WARSAW • BUDAPEST • AUCKLAND

Recycling programs
for this product may
not exist in your area.

ISBN-13: 978-0-373-29556-2

SIERRA BRIDE

This book is dedicated to my husband, Jim,
with much love and a grateful heart.

Available from Harlequin® Historical and
JENNA KERNAN

Winter Woman #671
Turner's Woman #746
The Trapper #768
Wed Under Western Skies #799
"His Brother's Bride"
High Plains Bride #847
Outlaw Bride #883
Sierra Bride #956

Oh, hard is the fortune of all womankind
She's always controlled, she's always confined
Controlled by her parents until she's a wife
Then a slave to her husband for the rest of her life.

~American Folk Song: The Wagoneer's Lad~

Chapter One

Sacramento, 1862

The only difference between the women on the street corners and Kate Wells was that she only had to sell herself to one man.

His passing was a mixed blessing. Despite the scandal and her resulting fall from grace, Kate did regain her freedom as a result of his murder. And she much preferred her current work to the duty she had to perform in the marriage bed. Both kept her up at night, but she didn't feel the need to wash after working in the milliner's shop.

Tonight she had a full moon to guide her as she walked home along the American River.

Unfortunately, the moonlight and the lanterns from the riverboat also served to illuminate things that were best shrouded in darkness. The wide street was not as deserted as it should be at this time of night. Saturdays were always this way, men with money in their pockets and mischief on their minds.

Kate slipped a hand into her bag. As she hurried on, she groped about for the only useful gift her husband ever gave her. At last her fingers gripped the cold, pearled handle of the Derringer. She hunched around the weapon as if she guarded it instead of the other way around. Her shoulders ached from her labors. There weren't enough hours in the day to earn a living. Between the boardinghouse and the milliner's, she worked sixteen hours a day and was still falling behind.

She glanced at the three women on the corner. Their bare shoulders and seductive postures advertised their business, and she wondered what they made in an hour.

One woman gripped the elbow of a scrawny man as she met Kate's gaze. It was like looking in a mirror. The confident pose, the false smile—Kate saw past all that and focused on the desperation glittering in the woman's eyes. She recognized the despair and it frightened her down to her bones.

Kate wasn't that hopeless yet, but it was a near thing, a nightly battle with the invisible line of respectability. Thus far she was only the widow of a thief. There were worse things.

Her gaze fixed on the crates just inside the alley. Steady gasping interspersed with grunts left little doubt as to what occurred just beyond her sight. She hugged her shawl tighter and hastened on. Her husband had made such noises when he pushed himself inside her. She squeezed her eyes shut fighting to bury the memory.

As she approached the next alley, she heard a different sort of sound. Something crashing and then cries of glee.

"That's got him!" someone shouted.

She glanced between the buildings and drew up short at the scene. Two men and a woman were rifling through the pockets of a large man who struggled to rise from the packed earth.

Kate's first impulse was to scream for help, which she did with gusto. This caused two burly men to stop offloading the steamer and to turn their heads in her direction. They came at a run. With this backup she charged into the alley herself. The villains looked so startled they simply stared.

The young woman held a black leather billfold.

Kate showed her pistol, thrusting her arm out before her like a sword. "Drop that right now!"

The woman didn't, but instead turned and fled down the back end of the alley and out of sight.

The men held their ground.

"What are you going to do with that, deary?" said one man taking a step forward.

"Stop or I *will* shoot you."

He didn't. She did.

The sound of the gun report was amplified by the narrow space, echoing off the walls. Her attacker fell to the ground, clutching his thigh. His partner lunged at her, slapping her weapon away and seizing her wrist. His fist cocked back. Kate had time only to close her eyes and brace for the blow, which she heard but did not feel.

Opening her eyes, she found the man she had

defended now standing beside her with the thief lying at his feet. She stared in wonder at this man who had knocked his attacker unconscious with a single blow.

He drew his pistol then and aimed just as the two dockworkers arrived.

"Saw it! Saw the whole thing!" one shouted.

"Get that one," shouted the other. Kate turned to see the wounded man hopping around the corner as the two deliverymen charged past her after the fleeing man, taking their lantern with them.

Kate found herself alone in the alley with the man she had tried to rescue, and his unconscious attacker. The only light came from the lanterns on the steamers behind him so she could not see his face. But he was tall and broad with light brown hair. He wore the clothing of a laborer, a dark work shirt of some heavy weave and denim jeans. Over the lot he wore a long duster, as if he had ridden in on horseback. Had he come here with the woman?

Kate felt trapped as she faced him. He nudged the fallen man with his boot. The thief showed no flicker of movement, beyond the rise and fall of his breathing, so her companion holstered his sidearm and took a step in her direction. He swayed as if drunk, but she smelled no whiskey. He stooped and retrieved her silver, double-shot pistol. When he straightened, he had one hand pressed to his head and the other about her gun. He offered her the pistol in an open palm.

"Thank you, miss."

She plucked her derringer from him and was stuffing it into her bag when his hand fell heavily on her shoulder. She screamed and then realized that he was not attacking her, but rather falling.

Kate managed only to guide his fall while she crumpled beneath him. As he lay half-across her lap, she stared at his attacker's boots, noting the tacks of one heel showed through the worn leather. She adjusted her position so his head rested on top of her thighs. It was in the process of moving him that she discovered a lump on the back of his head the size of a darning egg.

She prayed he had not split open his skull as she searched for any sign of blood, but found none. She pushed his thick hair back from his pale face. "It's all right now. I'll take care of you."

His eyes fluttered open and he stared up at her with childlike wonder.

He blinked. In the dim-filtered light, she first noticed his neatly trimmed side-whiskers, slightly darker than the hair on his head. He wore no beard, which allowed her to admire the clean sweep of his strong jaw and the fullness of his bottom lip. It was parted slightly as he drew long breaths. His thick, high brows lifted above gentle eyes and a broad straight nose. All in all, he was an exceedingly handsome fellow. His stare did something to her, making her skin tingle. It was a feeling long forgotten, the feeling of a girl attracted to a boy without knowing the heartache that would bring. Yes, this one was handsome and that made him dangerous. She straightened her spine and chided herself. She, of all people, should know better.

He whispered something, but she could not make it out, so she lowered her ear closer to his lips.

She listened, but still could not understand. She hovered over him, inches from his lips.

"Lie still now until help arrives." She hoped it would arrive and glanced in the direction that the two dock-workers had vanished.

He lifted a hand and threaded his fingers in her hair like a lover and drew her down toward him, kissing her on the lips.

She was so startled she could not think and then it was too late to think. His mouth slanted over hers, coaxing and stirring. Her stomach fluttered at this tantalizing moment of forbidden excitement.

The sound of the rapid strike of boot heels brought her to her senses and she drew back. His eyes drifted closed, but now a devilish smile curled his lips.

She stared down in mute horror at what had just happened, and then Kate blinked up at the swinging lantern held by one of the men who had come to her aid.

He stooped before the thief. "Still breathing." He glanced up at her. "How's yours?"

She stared down at his reclining body and the bulge evident in his britches and flushed hotly. Had the man not seen her kiss him? She cleared her throat. "He's swelling, his head, I mean—his head is swelling, from the blow." Trying to recover from her blunder, she pointed at the lump. "Just there."

The man squatted. His large hands groped the unconscious man's scalp. He raised his eyebrows and she knew he had found it. He gave a low whistle.

"That's a beaut."

"Where is your partner?"

"Brother," he corrected. "With the one you clipped. Dragging him back, but I wanted to be sure you was all right."

Kate smiled her gratitude. "Thank you for coming when I called."

He shrugged. "Lady in need." Then he looked at her, really looked, from her bonnet to the hem of her gown. "Why you out so late, miss? If you don't mind my asking—this is no place for a lady."

"I work for a milliner, extra hours, extra pay."

He nodded, wiping his big hands on his trousers. "I'm doing much the same myself, except the milliner part."

They shared a smile. It faded and died leaving a long uncomfortable silence.

"Should I go for help? Call the authorities?" he asked.

"Yes, I think so."

He turned to the would-be thief who still lay sprawled on the ground. "He don't look good." He stooped before the man. "Jaw's busted. Breathing though."

He hauled the man to his feet and tossed him over his shoulder with an ease Kate found frightening.

"You'll be all right?"

"Yes, of course."

Still he lingered, looking back up the alley perhaps for his brother before glancing back at her.

Kate smiled and patted her reticule. "Still have a shot left."

The man nodded his approval and lowered the lantern, leaving them in a pool of light. "My brother'll be along directly."

"I shall keep watch for him."

He strode off, moving quickly for one of such girth. The unconscious man flopped like a dead carcass on his back.

The fellow resting on her lap stirred and she returned her attention to him in time to see his eyes open. He stared up at her with beautiful pale brown eyes, as warm and inviting as sunlight through amber glass.

"Welcome back," she murmured, flushing as she wondered if he would recall the kiss.

He tried to sit, flinched and then fell back panting and pale.

"My head is splitting. What happened?" He spoke without opening his eyes. "I heard a woman scream."

"That was me."

He cast a sidelong look at her. "No, miss. Not you. I'd sure remember that pretty face."

"Who, then?"

"Dunno. She didn't say…" He flushed. "We got out here and two men grabbed her. They were…" His words fell off as he glanced at Kate.

"Go on," said Kate, trying to appear unruffled but feeling her face grow quite hot.

"I got her clear of them and—that's the last thing I remember."

"Perhaps *she* was the one who struck you." Unable to help herself, Kate stroked his forehead.

"Thanks for taking care of me, ma'am."

"I think you rescued me."

His eyes widened. "Did I?"

"You struck that other man after he attacked me. Don't you recall?"

He shook his head in dismay, then winced at the

movement. She gave his shoulder a reassuring squeeze and immediately regretted it. Her touch revealed just how solid and masculine he was beneath that overlarge coat. She drew back her hand and his smile faded.

"They're going for help." She stared, admiring his fathomless eyes. "Just rest now."

"Wouldn't move on a bet," he said, relaxing back into her lap.

"Are you dizzy?" she asked pushing his hair from his forehead and checking his eyes. They were clear and bright, with creases at the corners quite free of the tan that covered his face. This man spent his time out of doors.

"If I am, it's from looking at you."

She smiled at the pretty flattery. The man was a born charmer. For the first time, she considered what a picture they made in the alley, huddled together like sweethearts at a church picnic.

She tried to draw her hand back, but he captured it and planted a kiss on her gloved palm. She could not even feel his lips, but the thrill of his action made her stomach flutter. He did not stop at that but found the pulse point just between the edge of her glove and her sleeve and kissed her there.

Kate gasped and their eyes met, locked. She noticed the small gold speckles in his wide brown eyes and decided they looked more like amber flecked with mica.

After the bump on the head he'd suffered, she could not find fault. It made people funny. She had seen a neighbor boy fall from his back steps and for two days he wept at the drop of a hat. He was a brave boy, too, and not prone to tears.

"You saved my life," he whispered.

She laughed. "I could not even save your wallet."

He released her and patted his coat where his wallet should have been.

She withdrew her hand, chagrined that she did not ask him to release her and only withdrew now because he had recalled his losses. The man was distracting, to say the least. It was almost as if she was the one who had been struck on the head. Kate wondered if he could sense the wild beating of her heart.

"I'm sorry about your money."

He lifted a hand in dismissal. "More where that came from."

How very cavalier, she thought, for a man who had nearly worn through the knees of his trousers, but she kept silent on that matter. Perhaps he had drunk most of his pay before he was waylaid.

"Is your head aching?"

He closed his eyes a moment and nodded. "Stomach is bad, too. Feels kind of whoopsy." His eyes met hers. "Might be just 'cause you're sitting with me."

She laughed. "You are a devil."

"And you're an angel."

Kate returned his smile, feeling her heart beating in her throat. What was going on here?

He was mooning after her. She knew she needed to squash this immediately. She didn't encourage gentleman callers and saw no point in beginning a journey she had no desire to complete. Instead, she filled her days with her responsibilities at her aunt's boardinghouse, the piecework she took in and seeing to her sister's needs. God willing, things could continue on as they had.

Before she could set him straight, he made an effort to rise, reaching his knees and wobbling badly.

"Oh, careful now." She clutched his arm, keeping him steady.

"Everything's spinning." He leaned heavily against her, pressing one hand to his head. "Did I kiss you?"

She gasped, hoping he would not recall that.

"Yes."

"I'm sorry, ma'am. I'm right out of my head."

"Accepted."

They were silent a moment and then he said. "But you kissed me back, didn't you?"

She made an uncomfortable sound in her throat and nodded. "You rather took me by surprise."

She had never been kissed like that and certainly never responded in that way. Something about this man heated her skin like August sunshine.

His smile faded as his gaze grew more intent. The look he gave her stopped her breathing. For just a moment she thought she should run. But that was foolish. He was injured, surely he was no threat. But those eyes said otherwise.

"What is it?" she whispered.

"I'm going to kiss you again."

Chapter Two

It took the howling cry of a man to stir Sam Pickett from that kiss. He drew back to find his angel leaning heavily against his chest, her face tipped back and her mouth still moist. He knew he would never forget that sight for as long as he lived. He had to fight the impulse to gather her up in his arms and run off with her. How had she managed to do that with just the pressing together of their lips?

She blinked up at him and then cocked her head, becoming aware of the shrieks and curses. She drew back and they turned in unison in the direction of the approaching caterwaul.

A burly man, with arms like ham hocks dragged a bleeding, limping man by the collar of his ragged coat. Sam recognized the wounded man as one of the two who had waylaid him and rose to face them. He swayed dangerously. It was only by the quick bracing of the woman, now at his side, that he kept from pitching forward. Somehow she managed to keep him on his feet by clutching his waist. As he stood with one arm draped across her shoulders, he felt dizzy and sick as a drunkard on Sunday morning.

"Cork that pie hole," growled the man's keeper. He spotted them now and grinned, shaking the man by the collar like a terrier shaking a rat. "Caught one!"

The "one" in question screamed again and gripped his leg with both hands.

The thief lifted a bloody index finger, aiming it at the woman. "She shot me! That one! Her!"

At this, his captor cuffed him on the back of his head, sending his prisoner's greasy black hat careening to the ground.

"Ought to get a medal, you ask me."

Sam blinked at the woman. "*You* shot him?"

She eased away and he managed to retain his balance.

"I ordered him to unhand you first," she said.

He could only stare in wonder. All he could remember was waking to see one of the two thieves attacking this woman an instant before he'd landed a solid punch to the man's jaw. Then two other men barreled past and his mind went fuzzy again.

Sam assumed that the burly man had done the damage. Another thought hit him, a more disturbing notion. Were they a couple, these two?

He addressed the grinning man. "Do you know each other?"

"Screamed, she did. And me and Lans come a-running." He craned his neck. "Where is he?"

The bleeding man continued to howl.

"Shut up," shouted his captor. Then he turned to her. "Where's my brother?"

"After the authorities."

He nodded his approval. "Best get to the street." He addressed Sam. "Can you walk?"

Sam was clammy and weak, but he nodded. The dull throbbing in his head grew into a slamming sledgehammer of a headache. Now he knew exactly how one of his metal mining spikes must feel after driving. He thought his eyes might pop from their sockets by the force of the blood pounding behind them.

She came to him again, wrapping her small, strong arm around his waist and propping him up like solid timber in a collapsing mine shaft.

He recalled something then, her lifting her weapon. The glint of silver and then the barrel flash. That was when the other man attacked her.

"Who are you?" he asked.

"Nobody."

She got him out of the alley. The emergence of the wounded man, protesting his innocence, began to draw a crowd.

The next few minutes were a blur. He recalled her face, someone laying him in a wagon. There were police. He told them there were three of them, two men and a woman. The next thing he knew they were lifting him onto a canvas stretcher and through a wide doorway.

"Easy now," said a young man with a gaunt and florid face.

"Where is she?"

"Who, sir?"

"The woman who saved me."

"You came in alone, mister."

Had he dreamed the whole thing?

The lights all about him receded until he was left with only a shrinking circle of light. He'd fallen down a well. The light went before the sounds, but finally those vanished, as well.

Since leaving the hospital, Sam's mood had gone from bad to worse. At the knock on his chamber door, he lifted the knife beside the washstand and turned.

"Jessup, I'll slit your throat, I swear."

"Not if I slit yours first," came the curt reply.

Sam relaxed his shoulders and he grinned. It was not his irritating butler but Cole, his best friend—his only friend. Sam wasn't good at friendships. He'd learned long ago that you couldn't rely on folks. Most of them gave too little and expected far too much. Cole Ellis was an exception, allowing Sam to keep some distance without taking offense.

Cole's arrival was the first good thing to happen since he'd blacked out in the woman's arms. Who was she? He had to find her. It was the reason he was shaving when he should be in bed nursing his headache.

Cole opened the door and glared at Sam, who lowered the knife and lifted the towel to wipe the patches of foam off his clean-shaven face.

"Passed your man on the stairs running like his hair was on fire." Cole thumped the newspaper against his thigh as he glanced back down the hall. After a moment he returned his attention to Sam. "What'd he do this time?"

"He wanted to shave me, like I'm some kind of invalid." Sam threw the towel onto the washstand. He didn't like the man sneaking around like a weasel after a ground squirrel. His frustration boiled over.

"Is it his business what kin I got? Is it?"

Cole said nothing to this, but his eyebrows lifted a moment. His friend knew little about Sam's past, and had taken the hint when Sam had failed to mention anything more than his place of origin. Nobody knew about his childhood and that's the way it was and would continue to be.

"Maybe he was just trying to strike up a conversation."

That hadn't even occurred to Sam. Maybe he'd overreacted. "He's a noisy pain in my ass."

Cole's scowl did not lift as he glanced about the room. "One of the richest men in Sacramento." His tone dripped with disapproval. "When are you going to buy some proper furnishings?"

Sam looked at the washstand with the fancy marble top that had come all the way from Vermont. It was more costly than anything he'd ever owned. A china pitcher and matching basin done up with pictures painted in blue all around the outside sat on the surface. Next he glanced at the bare mattress, goose-down pillow and coarse wool blanket. Maybe he should have a chair or two.

"I got a bed. What the hell else do I need in a bedroom?"

"Curtains, for starters. No wonder you don't bring any women here."

"I don't have them here because I don't want them here. Women are like dandelions—they take root anyplace and are near impossible to get rid of." It was at that moment that Sam recalled that right before his accident he'd left Cole waiting in the bar when he stepped outside with the woman he'd just met. It did occur to him that his friend's foul mood might have more to do with his disappearance than with window curtains.

The woman had been a bad choice, since she obviously had been bait and he had snapped at her like a hungry catfish. She was just his type, buxom and brunette. Served him right that she tried to split his head open before she'd fled the scene. He rubbed the lump and glanced at Cole.

"Sorry about last night."

Cole's mouth remained in a thin grim line. "Thought you said you'd be right back."

Sam lifted a hand in contrition. "Sorry."

Cole blew out his breath in a sound of disapproval. Cole had been happily married for over ten years, owned a lumber mill and was co-owner of the mine that sprang from the claim Cole had bought and Sam had worked when Cole was too bereaved to do much but drink and brawl. Funny him disapproving of Sam doing the same thing.

Only Sam wasn't grieving over a woman. His scars went back further than that.

Sam just couldn't keep down his cynicism over Cole's happy marriage. He kept waiting for things to fall apart but they never had. Since surviving two winter rescues up Broadner Pass and a trial for horse theft, his friend had led a charmed existence.

Cole kept trying to get Sam to visit more often but

all the kids made Sam uncomfortable. It was so different from what he recalled of childhood.

Cole moved, with a grace that belied his size, stopping at the open window and peering out. "What was her name?"

"Never got it." Sam dropped his gaze. "It was a setup." He glanced up and saw the muscles in Cole's mouth tighten. "Two fellers tried to jump her in the alley, so I dragged the girl behind me to face them. You'll appreciate this part. The next I know, I'm lying on my back and I hear a gunshot."

"She shot you?"

"Blackjack, I think." Sam turned his head, pushing his hair out of the way to reveal the lump. Cole stepped closer and a growl escaped him. Sam faced his friend. "Now I see a second woman, a real beauty, fighting with a man over a silver gun. She shot his partner right through the thigh. Anyway, I punched him."

"Then what happened?"

Sam recalled the satin of her lips, the sweet taste of the deep recesses of her mouth and the passion that he'd only dreamed of, all of it there before him for just an instant. He wanted more.

"Don't remember."

Cole's eyes narrowed. "Like hell."

Sam couldn't keep the smile from his lips.

"Do you remember *her* name?"

"Never said."

"Do you remember my name?" asked Cole.

"What?"

"Because, I'm wondering why you didn't mention it

at the hospital." Cole thumped the paper against his open palm now.

How had he found out so quickly? The answer came a moment later when Cole tossed the newspaper on Sam's bed revealing the headline, Elijah S. Pickett Hospitalized After Attack.

"You should have sent someone for me. My God, Sam, you can afford the best doctors, the best of everything now."

He knew that in his head, but he remembered who he really was, down beneath the gold veneer. Deep below, he was still that unwanted kid who'd do whatever it took to survive. That, at least, had not changed.

But last night he'd tasted something better and he wanted more.

"I need to find her."

"Who?"

"The one with the derringer. The one with the bullocks to walk into that alley."

"Women don't have bullocks and how do you know she wasn't one of them?"

He'd seen her in that alley, a thrilling combination of fury and terror. No one was that good an actress.

"She wasn't."

Sam knew he sounded defensive and Cole gave him a wary look. They hadn't fought since the death of Cole's first wife, after the wagons had gotten bogged down in that blizzard. They'd tried walking out from Broadner Pass, but when Cole's wife had laid down to die, Cole had, too. Sam had heard him promise to go back for their daughter and so, well, it hadn't come to blows, but only because they were already too weak for that. Sam squeezed his eyes shut, forcing the memory down deep and hoping that this time it would stay there forever, but he knew it wouldn't. "I'm sorry."

"You know what she was doing in that alley?"

"Nope."

"She know who you are?"

"Nope."

"That'll change things."

It always did. Men wanted to be him and the women, well, they just wanted him. He was one of the richest men in Sacramento and owned the richest mine in California. Money allowed him to take what he wanted and not feel guilty about it afterward. It also kept him clear of snags, like marriages.

Cole waited while Sam finished dressing. "You give any thought to the Central Pacific?" Last night, Cole had proposed closing the pass and putting a railroad up over the mountain.

He had. That and the woman had been all he had thought of. He stared at Cole, reading the hopeful, eager expression.

"It'll work," Cole said. "With your backing, it'll go."

Closing that pass would be the achievement of a lifetime. Maybe attacking that mountain with steel rails would fill that dark, cold pit that still ate at him. Since surviving the ordeal, he had been throwing himself at those mountains. Robbing her of her wealth and burrowing through her like a cancer. But to reach right up over the top of her and set down a railroad track, that was grabbing the she-bitch by the horns, by God.

"Yes," Sam said with a conviction that surprised him. He was completely ready to throw everything he had at the Sierras, unfeeling bitch that she was.

Cole's face lit up with delight. "I'll set up a meeting of potential investors at the Sterling Hotel. You'll be there at two o'clock, right?"

That would give him the morning to find her. He drew on his coat, aiming for the door. "Sure."

"Newspapermen are waiting in front."

"Guess we go out the back."

"Where to?" asked Cole.

"The police."

"That can wait."

No, it couldn't. He wanted her address, now.

Sam waited as a police officer wrote out the address for a Katherine Wells on the back of a calling card, using a bottle of blue ink and a pen that skipped. Sam nodded his thanks and departed, feeling hopeful for the first time in months.

He easily found the address in a respectable but shabby part of town. He grinned at the sign before the premises. It read: Mrs. Maguire's Boardinghouse. If Miss Wells was a resident within, she was most likely unencumbered.

That suited him fine, because families unsettled him and he didn't fancy trifling with a married woman.

He had dressed in one of his new suits. It was Cole's idea to buy them, saying that potential stockholders would be more likely to fork over their money to a man who looked important. He tugged at the stiff collar. The railroad venture would necessitate more investors than he had ever needed for the mine.

If he had his way, he'd build the damn thing alone, but that wasn't possible. It was his misfortune that what he wanted most in the world would require him to wear a necktie.

He mounted the steps and stood, hat in hand, upon boards that needed shellacking. Large window boxes of white flowers lined the railings, making the dilapidated house seem more inviting.

Sam lowered his head to gather himself, trying to think of what to say to Miss Wells. Never before had he worried about making impressions. If a woman didn't care for the cut of his coat or the color of his eyes, he moved on. That happened less and less often as his fortunes changed. He had not approached a proper lady in ages, though he'd lost count of the ones who had approached him. Suddenly he found himself wanting something that he might not have the good fortune to possess. Perhaps that accounted for why his heart slapped against his ribs like a live trout tossed in the bottom of a rowboat. He didn't like the old feeling of helplessness creeping inside him like poison.

"The hell with this." He turned around as the door opened.

There stood an older woman, wiping her flour-coated hands on her long apron. She would have been attractive, except for the deep worry lines that flanked her mouth and the fact that she was thin to the point of being painful to look at. Her smile seemed genuine.

He stepped back a respectable distance and removed his gray Stetson.

"Mr. Tobin?" she asked, and then gave a hopeful smile.

That caught him off guard. "No. I'm sorry. Were you expecting someone?" He pressed on without giving her a chance to answer. "I'm looking for Katherine Wells."

"She isn't here. Is she expecting you? She didn't mention anyone."

"Who is it, Aunt Ella?"

The woman turned toward the parlor then back at him. "My youngest niece. Ears like a rabbit, that one."

Mrs. Maguire's smile deepened the lines in her careworn face, changing them to something welcoming. She stepped aside and swept a hand before herself. "Please come in, Mr...."

"I'm Elijah S. Pickett, ma'am." He stepped inside, gripping his hat before him.

"My niece is running some errands. You are welcome to wait." She paused as if only just hearing him and then she gave the reaction he had hoped for. "Did you say…?"

He nodded.

"My stars."

Sam's confident smile faded as he realized he had only just heard what *she* had said. She had said *niece*. That meant that Miss Wells was…damn it to hell, she didn't board here. She lived here and had a family.

He backed up a step, bringing him closer to the open door, having decided not to wait or even come back until he learned what kind of a woman he was pursuing.

Mrs. Maguire glanced down the front steps and her face registered surprise. "Why, there she is! Kate!"

Chapter Three

Sam whirled and saw her. All apprehension vanished at the sight of her and he broke into a broad smile. "There's my savior."

Katherine Wells stood frozen with one small foot perched on the lowest step and a basket of ripe peaches on her arm. She was just as he'd remembered her, only now, in the daylight, he saw the hair beneath her prim bonnet was as curly as a wood shaving and the color of his favorite chestnut mare. She was again dressed like a proper lady, with gloves and shawl. If they hadn't shared the most magnificent kiss of his entire life, he'd assume from the innocent look of her that she was inexperienced. Her simple cotton dress and absence of jewelry told him she came from humble roots, though not nearly as Spartan as his.

He descended to her and extended his hand, hoping her glove would mask its sudden dampness.

"What an unexpected surprise," she said.

She did look overcome, judging from the sudden pallor and the way she drew her lower lip nervously through her strong white teeth. That last gesture made Sam's mouth go as dry as a man three days in the desert.

Surprise, she had said. Sam wondered just what sort of surprise she found it as she rapidly withdrew her hand and backed away as if he were a molester of women. Her gaze darted from her aunt and back to him.

"You seem quite recovered," she said.

Her voice was sweet and lilting but held a note of apprehension. He gazed down into eyes a perfect mix of green and gray and found he'd lost the ability to speak. He stood staring like a stick of wood. Was she also remembering their kisses? Those sweet kisses had brought him to her as soon as he could walk a straight line.

He moved closer, catching the fragrance of cinnamon and fresh peaches. She stepped back, drawing the basket between them as if it were a shield, and glanced at her aunt.

"You recall my adventure of last evening? This is the man who was attacked."

"My stars," said Aunt Ella.

"I've come to express my gratitude," he said. *And to see if my savior is as lovely as I recall.* She was, more so, for hers was a beauty that can only be truly appreciated in the daylight. He saw in her a rare mingling of vulnerability and strength. *My God,* her skin looked perfect as a bowl of fresh cream. She was the kind of woman men would travel fifty miles overland just to have a look. Just the sort he needed at Dutch Flats. He could take her up to the mining camps and combine business and pleasure.

"Won't you join us in the parlor, Mr. Pickett?" asked her aunt. "I'll make some tea."

He dragged his gaze from Miss Wells to glance at her aunt. He hated tea for its bitter taste and color that most resembled dirty dishwater and he hated the idea of being trapped in a parlor across from this woman's guardian while trying to hold a cup that was as fragile as an eggshell. Why didn't women drink out of good enameled tin, he wondered, even as he forced a smile and nodded his acceptance of the offer. He must have cracked open his skull. That was the only explanation, because he was taking Katherine's basket and following the women into the house.

He would have followed her anywhere if it meant spending a few more moments with this woman. Her aunt reclaimed the peaches and excused herself before retreating down the hall and out of sight.

Sam had the sudden urge to pull Kate into his arms, but as he moved toward her, he heard the rustling of skirts just before a slim girl appeared in the doorway to the right. The unnatural tilt of her head and the dark glasses told him she was sightless.

She tipped her ear toward them instead of her eyes. Her curly hair reminded him of Katherine's but it was pale as moonlight. She looked to be somewhere between ten and twelve, and was already as pretty as a bug's ear.

"Kate?" she said, holding out a hand.

"Here, Phoebe." She moved to the younger girl and clasped her hand, tucking it into the joint of her elbow and drawing her forward.

"Mr. Pickett, this is my sister."

Good Lord, first an aunt and now a sister. He slid the thick felt brim of his hat through his fingers, sending it into a slow spin. This was not what he expected.

Kate stood beside her sister who now extended her small, pale hand. Did the girl ever go out?

"May I present Phoebe Jane Maguire. Phoebe, this is Mr. Pickett."

He shook the hand, marveling at its perfect form, in miniature. He avoided children, as a rule, especially thin, pale ones. But she was well dressed in a clean pale blue cotton dress, a white lace petticoat, bloomers that reached her ankles and a pair of kidskin slippers.

He released the child's hand and stepped back.

"He's big," Phoebe said to Kate.

However did she know that from a touch?

He held his smile, only belatedly realizing the child could not see it. He frightened children, mostly. Did they somehow sense his imperfections? After all, he had lived every child's nightmare.

Sam now registered what Kate had said. Her aunt was Maguire, her sister was Maguire. Why would she have a different name than her sister? The most obvious reason struck first and he glanced at her left hand, but it was still sheathed in the glove. His heart sank.

Was she married?

"Maguire?" he muttered. "But…"

She must have read his confusion, so poorly disguised. "I am widowed, Mr. Pickett, just a year past."

"I'm so sorry," he said automatically, but he wasn't, not by a mile. Widows were a whole different class.

They had experience and little reputation to protect. And if you were discreet, they tended to be more adventurous. Plus, they knew what a man wanted and were more inclined to give it to him.

No, he wasn't sorry by a mile. In fact he felt inclined to dance the jig he performed each time he had found a sizable gold nugget. She was a widow and alone over a year. Things were looking up.

He cast her a heated glance and she looked away, leading her blind sister into the parlor. Sam followed behind.

"Won't you sit down, Mr. Pickett." She indicated a dark pink settee.

He lowered himself into a lumpy mess of springs and horsehair. Beneath the worn fabric one spring in particular made a sizable impression. He shifted his seat, thinking he'd be more comfortable sitting on a rock pile.

The sense of unease at the unfamiliar threatened to sink him again. Likely she'd see right through him.

He glanced at the lace doily on the armrest, which was fixed in place with straight pins, and next to the side table, three porcelain figurines from the Orient glared at him. The room was a booby trap for a blind girl, but Phoebe left Kate's guidance and negotiated it like an experienced riverboat captain avoiding shoals and underwater snags. She slipped silently across the room making straight for a hard-backed chair. He was about to warn her of the knitting needles and yarn upon the seat, but she scooped them up as if sighted. The only indication of her condition she made was the slight reassuring pat she gave the armrest before sitting. Then she lifted her needles and began to knit with lightning speed. Phoebe disconcerted him by knitting while seeming to gaze straight at the ceiling.

"May I take your hat?" Kate offered.

He hoped she wouldn't put it out of sight. He hated the idea of leaving it behind if he had to ditch and run, but he forked it over. She took it into the hall and returned without it.

Kate sat adjacent to him, tucking her legs beneath her chair. He drank her in. Her aunt had withdrawn and her sister could not see. He unveiled his eyes and watched her flush, showing him that she felt this connection as well as he did.

Why did she sit there pretending not to notice, trying to avoid glancing at him? He wanted to gobble her up, breathe her in like hot air on a frigid day, but instead sat stiff and immobile as one of those ridiculous statues on the mantel beside the clock. Where was the hellion he'd seen in the alley? There was no trace of her in this breathtakingly beautiful lady.

He drummed his fingers on his knee as the clock pendulum swung. How soon before she would accept him into her bed?

Absently he rubbed the lump on the back of his head.

"How are you feeling, Mr. Pickett?"

Hard as a stallion around a mare in heat, was his first thought, but instead he said, "Ma'am?"

"Your head? You were rendered unconscious, I recall."

"Oh, it would take a wedge and a ten-pound hammer to do my skull any damage."

She graced him with a smile and he was momentarily

stupefied. Then he remembered the man knocking her gun away, grabbing her arm.

He was on his feet in a moment and kneeling beside her. She drew back but he captured her hand. "They didn't hurt you, did they?"

Kate shook her head, but his instinct told him she was hiding something.

He pushed back her tight sleeve just far enough to reveal the purple bruises encircling her wrist. He exploded to his feet with a bellow of rage. Anger he did not know existed poured through him like molten gold.

"Kate?" called Phoebe.

Kate moved to her sister's side. "It's all right. He has just seen my bruises."

"What bruises?"

So she'd hidden them from her family, as well.

Her aunt rushed in from the dining room, clutching a vicious-looking hat pin before her like a dagger.

"It's all right, auntie," said Kate.

The woman's shoulders sagged as she lowered her pin. Kate explained the situation as Sam reined in a monster he had not even known lived within him. He had seen things, terrible things, and never had he felt the urge for vengeance blaze with such acute force. It jabbed him like a red-hot poker and clouded all sense of reason.

Her aunt released the tiny buttons at Kate's wrist, drew off the gloves and then rolled up her sleeves, sucking in her breath at each turn of the fabric. Her efforts revealed four perfectly formed purple finger impressions on Kate's forearm.

The red glaze descended again. He turned his back and found himself staring at Phoebe, who sat clutching her knitting as if it were a stuffed doll. Seeing the child huddled in fear had the effect of throwing a bucket of well water at his face. Shame filled him at having terrified her. He retrieved the ball of yarn that had rolled a good distance across the floor but did not dare return it for fear of frightening her further.

Kate was arguing with her aunt.

"You'll do no such thing," she said.

"But it might be broken."

"It's not."

He turned to see Kate wiggling her fingers as if playing the piano that sat between the sofa and the window.

"Katherine." Her aunt's tone turned authoritative.

The two faced off. Why was she so stubborn?

"Do you recall our earlier conversation?" said Kate.

Her aunt looked confused.

Kate gave her a look, trying to tell her something without speaking. "About our situation—with the boarders?"

The older woman seemed to understand this cryptic comment.

"For goodness' sakes, child. Dr. Jefferies won't expect payment today."

Kate glanced at Sam and, in her scarlet cheeks and neck, he read the mortification over her aunt's blunt words. This was about money, then. She had not sought treatment because they lacked the funds.

He was about to offer to pay and then recalled that a man could not do such things without insulting everyone.

It was another stupid social convention he did not understand. He had money and yet he was powerless to help her.

He tried anyway. "Mrs. Wells saved my life, the least I could do is fetch a doc."

"I told you," said Phoebe, who was following the strand of yarn to the ball he clutched in one fist. "I said he'd give you a reward."

"He most certainly will *not*," said her older sister.

Why hadn't he thought of that?

"I could very easily."

"I would not accept it."

How had this all gone so wrong? For a moment, he wished he was alone in the alley with her once more.

"Then perhaps you would allow me to escort you to dinner as a show of gratitude." He could arrange to have a physician happen by.

Kate stiffened and he knew that he'd made another mistake, but damned if he knew what this one was. How long did he have to sit across tea tables before he could take her out?

"That is most kind of you, but I'm afraid that won't be possible."

Damn, he hated proper ladies. Under ordinary circumstances he didn't stay where he was not welcome, no matter how lovely the woman. But there was something about Kate. This aloof poise was some kind of mask. And he'd keep coming back until he got underneath it again.

"Oh, Katie, no," said Phoebe, who now reached for her ball of yarn and scooped it from him as bravely as a kitten stealing a scrap from a bulldog's bowl.

But Kate set her jaw. Her stubbornness only made

him want to kiss her more. They were strangers and so she could not accept money or invitations, regardless of her wishes on the matter. But in that alley he had held a wildcat. Her two faces fascinated him.

Perhaps a challenge, then.

"Any woman willing to charge into an alley with pistols drawn is surely brave enough to accept a dinner invitation."

Her aunt gasped.

Kate's eyes narrowed. "I think you mistake me, sir. I am a respectable woman."

"I never doubted it. It is why I know you will accept my attempts to show my *gratitude*." He realized he put too much emphasis on the word gratitude, making it obvious that he wanted more.

Kate resumed her seat. "Then you don't know me at all."

"I do." He stared at her, watching her color rise and her eyes twinkle. She was changing into the woman of fire. It was only her obstinacy that kept her from accepting now.

"Please," he said, meeting her gaze as he remembered that instant in the alley when he took what he wanted without her permission and she had let him. He couldn't do that now. Here the choice to accept him was wholly hers and influenced by her family standing witness.

He must be crazy, for he could think of no less than two dozen women who would jump at the chance to dine with him, yet here he was courting a reluctant widow who looked far too young to be married in the first place.

He held his breath waiting. How long had it been since he cared so deeply about anything?

During those moments, he realized that he longed for

such a woman as this—a woman with fire in her blood and steel in her spine. What he could do with such a woman beside him!

With her by his side, the miners would be falling over themselves to buy railroad shares, just to impress Kate.

And then he saw it again, that flash of danger reflected in her eyes, that spark that had ignited between them when they first met. He hadn't imagined it. It was there.

She opened her mouth to speak and his breathing stopped. Her voice hummed like the strains of a harp heard by a dying man.

"My aunt runs this boardinghouse. I am needed at mealtimes, so it won't be possible. Thank you again for coming for a visit, Mr. Pickett. I am so pleased to find you recovered."

She was on her feet now, showing him the door. She actually gripped his elbow and marched him from the room.

When they reached the entrance, Kate extended his hat and he refused to take it. Her arm relaxed and the hat nestled in the olive-colored folds of her simple work dress. He had never thought to be jealous of his hat before, but now he wished he could trade places.

"Is it because we were not properly introduced?" he asked, his voice now low and gruff.

She shook her head.

"My reputation, then, is that why you will not see me?"

"Rather, it is mine."

He wondered if she had a reputation to protect or one that she had already lost. Now he was more intrigued than before.

"I don't understand."

She glanced away. "I am recently widowed."

He surmised this was a device to send him off, because she'd already told him her husband's passing was a year ago and here he was, a man of wealth begging her to go out with him. It was obvious from the cracked plaster above their heads and the frayed carpet that money was not rolling into this establishment.

Why, then?

Her uneasy shifting and downturned face all spoke of shame. Why would she no longer meet his eyes?

He reached for her instinctively, his fingers encircling her upper arm as he dragged her forward.

"It was that damned kiss."

She stared up at him in horror, as if he'd come upon her in her bath. Her beautiful mouth dropped open as she gasped.

"A gentleman would not mention it."

"If you know my name, you know I'm no gentleman."

"Is that why you came, because you recognized me? Did you assume I'd just go with you?" She tugged away and he released her, but his attention stayed focused on her full lips. They were soft, pink and damp. But in the alley, they'd been swollen from his kisses and her breathing had come in soft, needy pants.

Her words filtered through his desire. What had she done that she thought he would know her?

"Who are you?"

"My full name is Mrs. Lawrence Wells. My late husband was a land speculator."

The name clicked as he recalled the events of last

April. Yes, he knew the scoundrel, knew the miner who shot Luke Wells and who was later hanged for it. He recalled accounts of the child-bride in the newspaper and articles detailing the lavish extravagance of their short marriage. What would the miners think of her if they knew? His plans teetered on unsteady ground.

Her husband had been a rascal and a thief. Sam never met the beautiful young bride. But he recalled she was favorite fodder for the newspapers. Femme fatale, gold digger, the keen-eyed opportunist, the papers had painted her black. She had married a man for his wealth and then lost it all. She was beautiful enough to match the descriptions.

He glanced at the shabby house. She lived with her aunt and had a blind sister. The paper never mentioned that and now he wondered if she had married a scoundrel out of ambition or need. If it was ambition, she surely would have found a replacement for she had everything necessary to take her pick of the bucks.

Sam stepped back. He had no intention of being the second husband. Hell, he had no intention of being a first husband. Trouble was, he still wanted her.

He hesitated, glancing to the parlor. Phoebe was now tucked tight against her aunt's side, and the aunt stared at him as if he were a stick of lit dynamite.

He turned back to Kate. She extended his hat again, glancing up. Was that regret in her eyes?

"Goodbye, Mr. Pickett."

To be seen with *this* woman was to start tongues wagging. And while he actually enjoyed scandals, he did not enjoy playing the fool. He would appear to be exactly what he was, a man smitten by a woman who had intentions on his fortune. He accepted his hat.

A terrible thought crossed his mind, casting a long shadow. "Were you in on it?"

He hoped to never see such a look of betrayal again. Kate went pale. Her expression changed from regret to one of physical pain. The urge to embrace her was irresistible, but as he opened his arms she stepped back with the quickness of a hare. Her eyes glistened and he realized she was about to cry. Then she pressed her lips tight. Her nostrils flared in a look that bellowed of impotent rage.

She opened the door and stood aside, refusing to look at him. He wasn't aware of stepping out, but did notice the rush of air as she closed the door firmly in his face and bent the brim of his new Stetson.

Sam stomped down the front steps as he reshaped his hat, wondering why he felt guilty for upsetting *her.* He didn't get far.

At the street, he turned back toward house. Why was he walking away? She had a reputation, but so did he. And there were ways around looking like a fool. One obvious one came to mind. True, he'd never had one before, but really, who better than Kate Wells? He couldn't see how such an arrangement would damage her reputation much. Besides, he was fairly certain one night with her would not be enough.

He headed back up the steps and knocked. Kate threw open the door, glaring daggers. There was his hellion.

He smiled. "Will you at least step out onto the porch so I may have a private word?"

"I'd be glad to."

Her aunt appeared in the hallway.

Kate glanced back. "It's all right, Auntie."

She stepped over the threshold and closed the door, then filled her lungs with air, as if trying to calm herself, but only managed to get him to stare at her amble bosom.

What she could do to a man in a low-cut gown. It occurred to him, briefly that her first husband might have had similar thoughts when he used her to attract investors, but he pushed it aside. He was trying to build a railroad, not line his pockets through fraud.

"I have a business proposition for you."

Kate scowled.

"I need a woman—"

"I suggest you try the docks."

Now Sam was scowling. "You going to let me finish?"

"My apologies. It is not my custom to sit idle while I am insulted."

He drew a breath and held it, then spoke his mind, preparing to be kicked down the stairs.

"Perhaps it is an insult, but it's also a business proposal and I'd like you to hear it just the same."

She lifted her chin, increasing her haughty look. She still only reached his shoulder so her efforts to look down her nose failed. The glitter of defiance only made him want to kiss her more.

"I want to make you my mistress."

Chapter Four

Kate's head dropped a moment and then she met his eyes. The anger was now replaced with a look of such sorrow he took a step in her direction, intent on gathering her up in his arms.

She retreated and glanced to the parlor window some ten feet away to see her aunt standing guard like an old bulldog.

Her voice was a mere whisper. "I am not surprised you would make such assumptions about me, considering my past. But I now live a respectable life. I sew and clean and help my family run this house."

"A woman like you shouldn't be scrubbing floors."

She cocked her head. "It's honest work."

"Long way from where you were. I could help you with that."

"I have no doubt. But I have something now that you cannot buy from me, Mr. Pickett."

"I doubt that."

"I'm speaking of my independence. It was not until it was lost that I discovered how dearly I missed my liberty. I do not plan to be so careless again. Good day."

He leaned forward, bringing his mouth to her ear. "You're not rid of me. Something happened back there. You felt it, same as me."

She inched back to peer up at him.

"I'll see to your wardrobe, jewelry and a place to stay, with servants."

Her brow quirked. "I have a place to stay—my home."

He smiled, seeing he'd caught her interest. "I can't very well visit you here."

"I should hope not."

In the past his persistence had served him well. In his mind, this was no different. He wanted her. It was only left for them to strike a bargain. "I need you, Kate. Lady as pretty as you could be a real help to me up at Dutch Flats."

"What?"

"I'm heading there to wrangle up investors for the railroad. Like to have you along when I tell them how much the railroad will do for them."

Her eyes narrowed on him and he felt the thin ice beneath his feet cracking.

"Why?"

"Miners love a pretty girl. You'd keep their interest while we sell stock."

"And share your bed."

He smiled, letting his grasp soften as he drew his hand away in a long caress.

He leaned in to whisper in her ear. "We'd be good together, you and I. I can feel it."

* * *

Kate drew back and looked speculatively at him. How did he convey how much he wanted her without sounding like a madman?

Kate glanced toward the window to see her aunt's worried face distorted by the glass. Something about this man did make her heart race. She'd admit that much. And their kiss had done things to her, secret, shameful, wonderful things. But she was no longer a girl. She knew exactly what he wanted from her and the reality squeezed her pounding heart and chilled her blood.

He'd not have her. Why was she even tempted?

He leaned in and she stood her ground, trying to control her racing heart. The man exuded sex. She looked away in an effort to escape the fire in his eyes only to become more aware of his enticing scent.

His voice was low and full of resignation. "I usually get what I want."

How could he know it was the wrong thing to say? He had inadvertently given her the reminder she needed. She'd tolerate no more bullies in her life. She stepped back.

"I am so sorry to disappoint. But you shall not have me. Good day, sir." She did not succeed in escaping him for he captured her hand.

"Thing of it is, I think you want it, too. I'm just more honest about it."

"I fear I have somehow misled you in some way. I am not that sort."

"Every living, breathing person on this earth is that sort."

She made no response to that.

"Am I so hard on the eye?"

She reclaimed possession of her hand. "No, Mr. Pickett, quite the opposite. You're handsome as sin and quite the charmer. Add that to your money and I'd be a fool to refuse. But you see I have already made this mistake once. You are exactly the kind of man I have strived to avoid since my husband's timely death."

"You mean untimely."

"Do I?"

That stopped him. She smiled and slipped inside.

Sam's hand on the knob kept her from shutting the door on him once more. "I'll be leaving day after tomorrow. If you change your mind, send word or come round to my place on I Street."

"Remove your hand, please," she said, her voice as gentle as a lamb but her eyes flashing fire.

Damn, he wanted her.

"Yes, ma'am."

This time he leaned back to preserve his hat brim, but she only closed the door with a firm click.

He smiled at her through the glass and damned if she didn't smile back. It was the smile of a house cat smirking at a stray who was yowling at her from the alley but could not get in. The question was: Would she come out and play?

As he headed back to his offices, Sam couldn't stop thinking of Kate. She was so damn pretty, beautiful really with a quality of daring he'd never seen in a woman. She had entered an alley alone to help a stranger and had just slammed her door on one of the wealthiest men in the city. He shook his head in bewilderment. Her capacity for spitting in the eye of the devil himself was arousing as hell. But she was having no part of him.

Then why had she kissed him as if she were dying for him?

He reviewed his other options and found fault with each female who came to mind. He had his heart set on Kate. He wasn't through yet.

He walked unseeing until he heard someone calling his name.

He turned to find Cole trotting across the street, dressed like a proper businessman right down to the little black tie he had knotted at the neck of his pristine white shirt.

"I liked you better as a mule skinner," muttered Sam.

"And I liked you better when you could tell time."

"What?" Sam reached for the gold pocket watch Cole had given him.

"You promised to come to the planning meeting for the railroad. You said you'd be there."

"When was it?" He checked the open watch face, trying to understand where the afternoon had gone.

"Two hours ago."

He met his friend's gaze. "I'm sorry."

"You are that, more and more often. Let me guess, a woman, again?"

"*The* woman."

Cole guided him toward a restaurant in the Sterling Hotel, just one block away. "Come on, tell me on the way. I'm meeting Bridget for dinner. Join us."

Sam dug his heels in. "The kids?"

"She doesn't generally leave them lying about since they tend to set things on fire."

"Charming. I'll walk you there."

"But you won't come in."

"Kids make me itch worse than chiggers."

Cole started walking and Sam had to hurry to catch up.

"So you found your little sure-shot?"

Sam scowled and then told Cole everything. When he finished they were no longer walking, but standing face-to-face on the street corner.

Cole pushed back his hat and gave a low whistle.

"Well, say something," said Sam.

"You say she has a family? I'm shocked you even crossed the threshold. That's not like you."

"You didn't see her."

"That's true, but she actually slammed the door in your face?"

Sam removed his hat and showed Cole the dented brim. Cole winced.

"You know about her?" asked Sam.

"I read the papers."

"Tell me what you recall."

Cole adjusted his tie. "Well, she was on the young side to be married. The papers called her 'Baby Kate' and he dressed her up like a living doll and showed her off. You had your head in a mine shaft about then, so you might not have seen her. But I did. She was stunning. I know you met her husband. He approached you, about a land deal. Didn't he?"

"Stank to high heaven. I knew he never owned that land.

Selling fake deeds and leaving others to sort out the details. Small wonder Keiler put a bullet between his eyes."

"Papers called her a gold digger and when the truth of her husband's dealings came to light, they said she was in on it. Never proved in a court, but I guess she found out who her friends were."

Sam thought of the shabby little boardinghouse. Kate Well's rise and fall had been stellar. Sam knew the same could happen to him. Fortunes were easily won and lost here in the land of milk and honey. He felt the mountains' chill touch him again. Money was all the insulation he had. He needed it to ward off the nightmares that dogged him even now.

They reached the restaurant and Sam drew to a halt.

"You'll come in to say hello," insisted Cole.

Hello would turn into "have a drink" and then "order something." Sam ground his heel into the plank sidewalk before the hotel. Lately, more and more, Cole had been giving him that disappointed look.

He liked Bridget. It was just that he never knew how to behave. He had never been part of a family and so their intimate dealings made him nervous, as if he were peeking through a spy hole.

"I gotta go."

"Why does the sight of a baby send you into full retreat?" asked Cole.

Sam ignored him. "I'm planning to go up to Dutch Flats day after tomorrow. Drum up some investors and check on the trouble you mentioned."

"Be careful."

"Always."

* * *

"I think I'll move in with you two. Free up another room for a new boarder," said Ella, her voice a little too casual.

Kate's internal compass began to spin. Turning away from the dough she was kneading, she faced her aunt. "Is Mrs. Larson still in arrears?"

Her aunt's gaze didn't meet Kate's eyes. "I'm sure the check will arrive any day."

"Auntie, if she can't pay, she can't stay."

"Well, I won't just put her out. She has no one, not one soul in the world." Her aunt Ella had a habit of gathering strays and people without means. She collected them the way some people collected sea shells.

"She has a son. Why can't she move in with him?"

Phoebe rested her knitting on her lap. "Because his wife hates her. And her son, Arthur, hasn't sent her any money in over a month. She cried today after the post. I heard her."

Kate knew exactly how she felt. She turned to her aunt. "But you had enough for the mortgage this month, with what I gave you?"

Her aunt glanced away. "Nearly."

The creeping unease grew. This crawling battle to get by seemed more treacherous then darting into an alley after dark. Everything was plain there, the villains, victims and heroes, all taken in at a glance. Kate's world was much more unclear. Was her aunt at fault for taking in poor tenants, or the tenants for not paying on time or their sons for not sending the money with which to pay? Was it her fault for her poor choice of a husband, or her husband's for being a thief?

People imposed on Ella because of her kind heart and weren't Kate and her sister just another imposition? They were, after all, two more strays her aunt could not turn away.

"How short are we?" asked Kate, the dough suddenly forgotten.

"Oh, you're too young to worry over such things. I'm sure we'll manage if I move in with the two of you and we get another boarder."

"But let me pick him this time, Auntie, please." Kate's tone held poorly concealed frustration.

The only reliable resident was Mr. Porto, who paid on time and in full. Kate had found him. Mrs. Guthrie, her aunt's choice, generally ran a month arrears and Larson, well, she was even more hopeless than the three of them.

Kate's heart broke a little more. Perhaps she was being selfish. That morning Sam had made a proposal that would solve their financial worries.

No. Not again. She would not allow herself to be displayed on the arm of a rich, brutal man as if she were some trinket.

The last time she found herself in such dire straits she had been just sixteen and alone, with her sister to look after. Only fourteen short hours had passed between the fever and her mother's passing from cholera. Kate had not even had the coin to bury her. But Luke had. And he'd been interested, waiting only until after the funeral to make his intentions known. Stupidly, she had insisted on marriage, not realizing that a wife was trapped by her vows.

She never intended to let that happen again. Kate set

aside the dough and turned to face her aunt, hesitating
when she saw Phoebe sitting beside the stove.

"Phoebe, will you get my sewing kit? I need to darn
this stocking."

Her sister set aside her knitting and felt her way out
the door. Kate waited until the dining room door squeaked
on its hinge then turned to her father's only sister.

"Auntie?"

Her aunt would not meet her eye. That alone increased her apprehension.

"Hmm?"

"How much?"

Ella met her gaze, pressing her lips together and
scowling because she was pressing the issue.

"How much?" whispered Kate.

Ella stared down at her apron. "Eight hundred."

Kate wobbled and thumped against the counter, feeling like a fraying yarn doll whose knots had finally
come loose. Her vision blurred and a sheen of sweat
erupted on her skin.

Behind her, something clattered to the floor.

"Kate!"

She could never raise so much. She glanced at her
aunt and saw her coming toward her. She was
speaking, but Kate could not hear past the roaring in
her own ears.

All the honest work she had done. Not enough—not
nearly enough. It would happen again, just as it had after
her mother's passing, before she ever knew of Ella's existence, back when she had no options but one.

Ella gripped her shoulders now.

She turned her head and called to Phoebe. "Fetch a damp cloth, child."

"When is it due?" Kate asked.

Ella pressed her hands together before her as if about to pray, but then bit her knuckle. "It's past due. Ninety days past due. They're foreclosing at the end of the month."

Kate's knees gave way and she slipped to the floor, landing hard on her seat before the chopping block. Ella crouched before her.

Phoebe felt her way to Ella. "What's wrong with Kate?"

"She's feeling, um, unwell."

"When were you going to tell us?" whispered Kate.

Ella wiped Kate's face with the cool cloth. "I was hoping that with a new tenant, I might talk them out of it again. The bank doesn't want this drafty, old house. They want their money."

The cloth moved down Kate's neck.

"It's happened before," said Ella.

"Before," gasped Kate.

"Last Christmas time. Can you believe it? What kind of an establishment removes one from their home at that sacred time of the year?"

"But I brought them a hundred dollars and they stopped sending letters until now. Only this time they did put down a date."

Kate closed her eyes.

"What's happening?" asked Phoebe.

Kate ignored her sister. "Do we have any money at all?"

Ella hesitated only a moment. "None."

Phoebe began to cry.

Ella cradled Phoebe to her as she glared at Kate. "And that is precisely why I did not tell you."

Eleven days. How much would the bank accept and how would she raise it in only eleven days?

But she knew how. She would have to do it again, have to give herself to Sam, have to accept him pawing her, pushing into her. She squeezed her eyes shut, trying to banish the images of Luke folding her over a washstand and lifting her skirts over her head. Kate swallowed her pride and forced down her fears. She whispered the truth she could barely say aloud.

"I can't say no."

Chapter Five

Kate made it to her room before the tears started. They were angry tears, hot, scalding tears that took the fight from her drop by drop until she reached acceptance. There was no option but to become his mistress.

With dismay she noted her reflection in the mirror above her washstand. Her eyes were puffy, red and sad. She stared down at the faded cotton dress.

Kate straightened her spine and stripped out of her ordinary attire. Then she poured a pitcher of water into the basin, careful to turn the sharp chipped edge toward the rear, before splashing water on her face.

"If there was another way," she said to herself. She grabbed the towel and mopped her face.

Kate put on her Sunday dress sewn from narrow panels of pale green-and-cream-colored remnants. When she had finished the milliner called it more quilt than dress but admitted that none of the customers would recognize the origins. For it certainly would not do to have a seamstress appear in public in an outfit matching one worn by a paying customer.

It was not fine, but it was the best she had.

Kate had once had an enviable wardrobe, but she'd lost that and everything else when her husband's debts were settled.

She undertook her hair next, sweeping the long tresses into a loose knot at her nape. That was as close as she dared come to letting it down completely. Experience had taught her that men were enamored of long, loose hair and she needed every advantage before she went groveling to Mr. Pickett.

Kate tied her bonnet strings and tugged on her gloves. She thought of Sam's hands, holding her as if he owned her already, and waited for the shudder of revulsion that never came.

He had told her that they would be good together. A good match. Did he mean that she would be a benefit to his business dealings? But that did not explain his contention that she wanted him as much as he wanted her. It wasn't true—was it?

Still her stomach did flutter and her face grew hot as she thought of him. That had never happened before. And why did she look forward to their meeting instead of facing it with grim resignation?

"Madness," she said to the empty room.

She descended the stairs, pausing at the coat tree to don a shawl. She stared at her reflection one last time. A properly dressed young woman stared back. She did not look like a femme fatale off to a clandestine meeting with a lover. She just looked…sad. Her eyes were those of a much older woman, but Sam would not be looking there. He would look, as all her admirers did, bewitched by her figure and her face. Men always stared at her mouth as though it were something rare and delicious. Sam was no different.

Yet he *was* different, because he was the only one who ever made her want to kiss him back. In his arms, she lost her common sense and forgot all that her first husband had taught her about the foolishness of love. Sam gave her hope and desire at once.

How sad that tonight it would all come crashing to an end.

She knew what to expect and it would be humiliating at the very least.

But before that, she needed to strike a hard bargain. There was no other way.

She marched down the front steps and set off purposefully along the street, slowing as she mused on his kisses and the heaviness they had caused in her breasts. How, at the time, she'd had an irresistible longing to press up against him. She recalled the moisture she had felt between her legs as she kissed him and felt herself flush. It was as if her body knew things she did not.

What had he said? *Every person on this earth is that sort*. Was that true?

Here she stood, a year older and hopefully one year wiser, in exactly the same place she had been once before—in need of funds with a rich man willing to care for her. Only this time he did not offer marriage.

That was better, was it not? This way she could leave him if he proved cruel.

She would never again bind herself in marriage. Only fate had rescued her from that blunder. She might very well have been tied to that brute for life. No, she'd never again sell herself so cheaply. Certainly she could tolerate lying beneath a man, if she knew that there was an end in sight.

But a mistress. Once she did this thing, she would become all that they had earlier called her. Kate sighed past the heaviness in her chest and continued on. Her reputation was expendable. She would sacrifice it or see her family set out on the street like rubbish.

She could do nothing less to save Phoebe. It was her duty, after all.

It didn't matter that this time she knew the truth. Those pretty dresses and beautiful jewelry came at great personal cost.

Her husband had been as mean as a rattlesnake and after she discovered what was required of a wife, her initial affection had died a harsh death.

Her footsteps slowed again as she considered that Sam might be more dangerous than Luke, because her mind knew the truth, but her body still wanted him to kiss her.

She couldn't understand her longing. She had thought that marriage to Luke had killed that part of her. Last time, Kate had recognized her mistake too late. Luke was a different man in private, where he lost his jovial manner, his glad-handing and his humor. If it had only been the brutal taking of her body, she might have born it. But he'd also used Phoebe as a hostage to ensure his wife's compliance in the bedroom and in his business dealings. He'd been very careful to see that, while he dressed her in fine furs, satin and expensive jewelry, he allowed her no money and always kept her under close watch. She'd asked for an allowance only one. Kate shivered. After that, she'd considered hawking some of her jewelry, only to discover that he locked it up each night. His suspicion was justified. If she could have run, she would have.

She tugged at her gloves and marched on, like a general preparing for battle. The traffic on the street was heavy this time of day, with wagons coming and going from the livery and shoppers out running errands. She knew it was unseemly to arrive on foot, but she could not spare the cost of a carriage ride.

She passed the Coats Hotel and found, to her chagrin, that her steps faltered. It was the place where she'd first met Luke. He had glanced at her and then stopped dead. He'd been flirting with her when her mother arrived and embarrassed her by telling Luke that she was only fifteen. It had caused a quarrel between them because Kate had been so certain she was all grown up and had been flattered by Luke's interest. Now she looked back with the sure knowledge that her mother had been right on every count. He was a rogue and a drunkard and a gambler.

Her stomach growled at the intoxicating aroma of fresh bread emanating from the bakery, but she did not pause. Pressing her hand over her rumbling belly helped quiet it.

The neighborhood changed on 2nd Street. She assumed Sam's home would be impressive and so she walked away from the river. As she journeyed along, the shops gave way to homes of a grander and grander scale. She asked a gentleman on the corner of 22nd where she might find Mr. Pickett's residence and he described the building to her in detail. She did not expect to find many gates flanked with stone lions, so she continued confidently on.

Her confidence fled when she reached her destination. What if he was not at home or was not alone or he had changed his mind? What if he had not changed it? Would she be forced to bed him immediately?

Kate stood in the road on aching feet as the afternoon sun vanished behind her. The light of the setting sun gilded the iron fence surrounding the huge mansion.

Kate stared at the stone columns flanking the open wrought-iron gate stretching up twenty feet. The forbidding entrance contrasted sharply with her home that welcomed passersby with a cheery sign ringed with pansies.

The large stone mansion looked as if it had dropped from the sky onto this lot, for there were no trees, bushes, shrubs or flowers to soften the hard edges. In fact, the only thing growing was weeds.

"Oh, my," she said.

The structure was impressive, but somehow looked new and abandoned all at once.

Every window was ablaze with light, as if he were throwing a magnificent party, but the lack of window curtains made the house seem hollow.

She was beginning to feel the familiar nausea that she had not experienced since her late husband's death. It used to happen when he came home, stinking of whiskey and impatient with her efforts to feign sleep.

Kate began to tremble. It took everything she had to

not turn tail and run. Instead, she crept through the gates and up the granite steps to the massive walnut doors where she attempted to peer through the etched glass windows. She spied the bell and pulled it before she could completely lose her nerve.

The door yawned open.

"Good evening, miss." The pinch-faced man gave a brittle bow then turned to her without lifting his gaze to meet hers. He gave no indication that it was unusual to find a single, unescorted woman on the doorstep. That made her wonder how often he faced this same circumstance.

Kate wished she had paid more attention to the papers. But by the time Mr. Porto finally relinquished them, she was either too tired or engrossed in reading a story to Phoebe.

"Whom shall I say is calling?"

"Ah, it's Miss Wells to see Mr. Pickett. I have a card." She reached into her reticule, past the derringer and tortoise-shell comb, to retrieve one of the preprinted calling cards and extended it to him.

"Do come in."

He took her wrap and waited while she untied her bonnet strings and carefully secured the hat pins back into the crown.

The man held her hat and shawl and used the other hand to motion her to a seat in the entrance. So she was not to be shown into the parlor. It was a bad omen.

"I shall see if Mr. Pickett has yet returned home."

Of course he already knew, but Kate was well acquainted with the rules of this engagement. "Thank you."

Then she glanced longingly at the exit and took the

seat in the hall that he indicated. There she waited. Her mind wandered to the alley and their stolen kisses.

Was that anticipation fluttering about in her belly? How unexpected. She flattened her opposite hand over her corset stays and muttered, "Traitor," to her treacherous body. How could she long for him when she knew the humiliations involved when a man takes a woman?

The little thrill of being pursued wilted under the cruel reality. Luke had not waited for the marriage to take his due. The ring she wore in promise had given him license to her body and had it not been for Phoebe, she never would have seen the altar. She squeezed her eyes closed at the memory of the tearing sensation and the blood that smeared her thighs.

The pocket door, before her, crashed open. She jumped to her feet, sending her reticule swinging wildly from her wrist.

Kate concentrated on not toppling backward as she pressed her hand over her pounding heart. He'd nearly scared the life out of her.

Sam's big frame filled the doorway, his shirt untucked, his sleeves rolled to the elbow as if he could not even take the time to put on a jacket before seeing her. Dark hair dusted his forearms. The top two buttons at his throat were undone, giving her a clear view of the bulk of muscle on his chest. To appear before a lady in such a state was unacceptable. She was about to tell him so when she remembered. She was no longer a lady.

She gaped up at him, registering his liquid brown eyes, twinkling as he grinned at her.

"You came," he said.

He clasped her elbow and ushered her into the room, slipping the pocket door shut behind him. When she stood beside him, she recalled just how big he was. She clutched her bag before her, reassured by the small pistol secreted within. She should have met him in a public place, but the discussion they must have was so delicate it required privacy. Unfortunately, privacy allowed other things.

He released her and she stepped away.

"Did I startle you?"

She nodded, her hands pressed flat over her heart. "A bit."

He glanced toward the closed door and then back to her. There was no need to ask what he was thinking now. She read it in the flash of heat in those eyes and in the step he took in her direction.

"Have you changed your mind?" he asked.

He took another step toward her and she scooted to the end of the tête-à-tête chair. It didn't stop him. He just kept coming.

"I've missed you," he said. It had only been eight hours since he'd found her, yet somehow her whole world had changed.

He leaned forward, closed his eyes and breathed her in. His eyes snapped open and pinned hers. "You smell like lavender."

She blinked, overwhelmed by his eagerness. Could he expect her to seal the arrangement now? He moved closer and she squeaked as she retreated.

"I couldn't get you out of my mind." Another step brought him within inches. "I tried."

What did that mean? Had he been with another woman? She pressed her lips together and scowled, then wondered why she should care?

She leaned away as he leaned in.

"Did you miss me?"

The night of the the attack she had dreamed of him and awoken with her body humming like a teakettle about to boil. But she would go to her grave before she would tell him that. Nor would she reveal the warm ache his presence now evoked. He seemed to take all the air from the room, making her light-headed.

"Not at all."

He laughed. "Little liar."

He caught her wrist and tugged until she collided with his chest. He sat on the armrest of the expensive double chair. In an instant, he had her cornered between his splayed legs. She stood trapped, eye-to-eye with Sam.

She struggled for a moment, but to no effect. She briefly considered shooting him, but discarded the notion, heartwarming though it might be.

His strong arms held her firmly, neither drawing her in, nor releasing her, as if he was waiting for her to grow accustomed to this intimacy.

It seemed she would have to render payment immediately. Why had she thought Sam was somehow different than her late husband?

Her stomach tightened, but the dread she expected did not come. She liked the feel of his fingers splayed around her waist.

"Kate?" He stared at her with a singular attention that caused her to catch her breath. "I want to kiss you again.

Since I met you, I can't seem to think of anything but kissing you."

"Mr. Pickett."

"Sam." His voice was low and husky.

The sound did things to her insides.

"Say it. I want to hear my name on your lips."

His fingers rested on her bare throat and then glided upward until he'd taken control of her jaw. The contact caused her breasts to ache, bringing her nipples to tight, aching beads. She'd never experienced anything like this and gasped in surprise.

He lifted her chin and held her. She unveiled her eyes and stared at him, reading the hunger burning like a banked fire. His lips were close to hers, but he paused there, his warm breath fanning her cheeks. She gave a little moan of yearning. Why didn't he kiss her?

"My name," he breathed.

"Sam, oh, Sam, please kiss me again."

His lips descended in an act of possession. His tongue brushed her mouth, seeking entrance once more. She opened her lips and he drove forward, his tongue gliding along hers. He tasted of brandy and smelled of leather. She moaned again at the shot of desire that stabbed downward to the juncture of her thighs. His kiss deepened, rousing a throbbing ache like nothing she'd ever experienced.

His hands divided, one heading north to delve into her hair and cradle the back of her head. He controlled her and brought her forward so her aching breasts pressed against the wonderful hard muscle of his chest. The other hand moved south over the whalebone stays of her bodice and down to her bottom, where he gripped her and drew her forward, until her soft mount connected with the long hard erection. The contact was like touching fire. She jumped back.

He kept her from total escape, letting her draw away only far enough so he could see her face. His gaze seemed unfocused and his breathing came in ragged pants. When his attention snapped to her again, she saw the hunger as clearly as she felt her own.

"I can't get enough of you. Kiss me again," he ordered.

The order, so similar to what her husband would have said, washed cold over her. What was she doing? She wasn't one of his bar floozies to be pressed up against the wall of some alley. Not yet anyway.

Kate arched away as he pulled her forward, pressing her hands at his shoulders and straightening her arms.

"Release me, Mr. Pickett."

He did, surprising her so much that she staggered backward. He caught her before she could fall. She found herself pinned to his chest again, with her hands gripping his wide shoulders, feeling the hard temptation of his muscles and the uncomfortable lump of her reticule pressed between them. His muscles tensed beneath her fingers as he gripped her waist. She did not yield to temptation, this time, and stepped briskly away. He let her go.

"Business first, then," he said. "All right." He raked his long fingers through his thick hair and exhaled. When he looked back at her, he still appeared eager.

She sat in the opposite side of the tête-à-tête chair, taking advantage of the sinuous curve of wood and padding to force a separation between them. If he chose to sit beside her, he would have proximity, but they would face in opposite directions and, more importantly, be contained by the firm barrier dividing them. She clutched her bag on her lap and waited for him to join her.

He grinned at her but did not seat himself. Instead, he chose to lean against a ball-and-claw-foot table just before her. He folded his arms across his chest. The effect was to give her a startling view of his bare flesh at the gap of his shirt. Her heart now seemed to be beating in her throat.

"What are your expectations?" she whispered.

His smile spoke volumes. "Come with me on this trip to Dutch Flats, talk to the miners, warm my bed." He crossed his legs at the ankle. "Take meals with me when I'm free."

Here was a chance to strike. She lifted her eyebrows and tried to look bored. Her flushed, hot cheeks undoubtedly undermined her efforts to affect aloofness. "Anything else?"

"Should you be party to my business dealings, I'll insist on discretion."

"Agreed. And your offer?"

He smiled. "All the dresses you can buy, shoes, hats, carriage, driver, apartment, servants."

Just like Luke, he had not offered her an allowance. She opened her mouth to correct the omission, to tell him she needed eight hundred dollars outright, but was seized by a cold panic.

"Jewelry?" she asked, hoping he would want to show her off in something valuable and that he would not be quite as vigilant as Luke had been.

He laughed. "When I feel inclined."

"I should like something to seal the bargain, something that will assure me that you value our agreement."

His smile turned cold. "So would I."

She ignored this and forged on, wondering where she found the audacity to be so bold. "As I said, I cherish my independence—highly. This arrangement would have to be extremely tempting for me to entertain it. In addition, may I say that my reputation will most certainly suffer from this liaison."

"I should doubt it, as it is less than sterling."

She narrowed her eyes. "In any case, I will need to see to my own future when you grow tired of me."

His smile vanished. "Are you so certain I *will* tire of you?"

Now he was frightening her. Was this her next tyrant? Her confidence faltered. "I assume so. Isn't that the way with mistresses?"

"I don't know. I've never had the notion to take one—until now."

He stunned her speechless with this announcement. What made her any different than the others? Was it her reluctance that tempted him? That would not last much longer. Once the contract was struck, he would have what she had withheld. She was certain he would be disappointed. Luke always was.

Sam lifted one hand to rub his jaw as he studied her. "Well, then I'll pick out a piece to show you how much I value this arrangement. Pearls? Or do you prefer diamonds?"

She understood his calm now and her heart sank. "You are making fun of me."

"I'm not. I'd love to dress you up."

Her husband had loved that, too. It helped him distract the miners while he fast-talked them into buying claims he never owned. She was to be bait again. How she hated herself.

"I will accept your offer under certain conditions," she said, glancing at her bloodless fingers clenched in the fabric of her reticule.

He unfolded his arms and clasped the edge of the table at either side of his lean hips. She looked at the size of his hands, imagining them striking her across the cheek, and lost her nerve again.

He raised a brow at her hesitance. "Don't even think about denying me, Kate." He was on his feet again, making her feel small and vulnerable.

She leveled her gaze. "We both know what you want. But despite what you think of me I am not some common…"

He lifted a hand. "Don't say it."

She almost laughed at his unwillingness to hear her speak the truth, but said nothing further.

"I'll not misuse you. I'll see to your needs."

Her only need involved a separate bedroom and eight hundred dollars in ready cash.

"You'll sleep in my private car or apartments I provide for you. No one else will so much as touch you, I swear." He held his arms out now, as if offering himself to her. "And at severance, I'll buy you a house and provide a settlement to compensate for your sullied reputation."

She was so shocked she did not know what to say. He took her silence for hesitancy.

"The amount will depend on the length of our liaison and will be generous."

She stood and extended her gloved hand. "Very well then, Mr. Pickett. We have a bargain."

He clasped her palm to his, but instead of shaking, used it to spin her in a half circle, standing close, leaning in. His lips found her bare neck. She could not keep herself from leaning back against him as his kisses turned her body liquid. She felt the wetness between her thighs again and her eyes popped opened in surprise. What was this?

She leaned away from his sinful kisses only to feel his hot breath fan her moist skin.

His hand came around her, pressing the corset stays into her stomach to bring her bottom into contact with his hips. His arousal was large and unmistakable even through her many petticoats.

"Come upstairs with me."

Her body stiffened. She was not ready. The fear nearly blinded her. She glanced toward the closed door.

He must have read the change in her, for he drew away and turned her to face him, his expression strained.

"You don't trust me."

"Have you given me reason to?"

His eyes narrowed and her breath caught. She had overstepped, questioning his credibility.

He did not shout or throw something at her, as Luke might have done. Instead, his mouth quirked in a half smile.

"I'll send you something this evening."

Her eyes widened in understanding. He thought her hesitance was over his failure to complete the preliminary step in their bargain. She nearly laughed at the ease with which she would escape, until she realized how mercenary he must believe her to be. Perhaps she was, for she would not be here at all if he did not have what she needed.

She took advantage of his assumption. "I am sure you are a man of honor." She could not quite get that last word out, knowing that he had, in effect, purchased her services and that an honorable man would never place a lady in such a situation. "But a single woman must protect herself."

"Shall we seal the bargain?" he asked.

Kate's eyes widened and he laughed, then turned to a cabinet and retrieved a whiskey bottle and poured a drink. He lifted the bottle and his eyebrows simultaneously in offer.

"No thank you."

He stared at her with dark eyes over the rim of his shot glass then tipped it back, downing the liquor in one long swallow. Why did the sight make her mouth go dry?

He was so much like Luke, tall and strong, rich and lusty. But he was different, too, surprising her by not doing as she expected.

He blew out a breath and slapped the glass down with unnecessary force. She flinched.

Did Sam have a mean streak, too? The notion stole her desire, draining it away like water through a sieve.

She was experienced enough to know that a bed and a horizontal position were not necessary for coupling. It was one of the first lessons her brutal husband had taught her. She began to tremble.

"Make arrangements for your dresses at any shop you like and send me the bill. Go to a big one that's got things on hand and buy at least one riding outfit."

She nodded her acceptance of this, still unable to believe she had obtained a temporary reprieve.

"I'll see you at the train station day after tomorrow at eight in the morning. Don't wear any bloomers."

With that edict, he turned and stormed from the room, nearly throwing the pocket door off of its track as he passed.

What in the name of heaven had she done?

Chapter Six

Kate returned home after the long walk from Sam Pickett's gilded palace, hot, thirsty and demoralized.

She found her aunt in the kitchen, as always. "Did you see your Mr. Pickett?" Aunt Ella thumped the kettle back on the stove.

"I did." She looked about. "Where's Phoebe?"

"Back steps, feeding the stray cat. Tell me about your visit. He's such a handsome man."

He was, devilishly so. His wide shoulders and muscular frame made her fingers twitch to touch and explore.

"And he's rich," said Ella. "Owns a whole gold mine, the biggest one. Isn't that right?" Ella stroked Kate's cheek. "And look at you, pretty as a flower growing on a dung heap."

"I just want to stay here with you and Phoebe."

"Oh, nonsense. It's been over a year. And he fancies you, Kate. I know you must think me ancient, but I do recall the joys of a marriage bed." Ella met her astonished stare. "Clearly."

Had she said joys? It did not feel like joy with Sam, more like torment, an aching need unfulfilled.

"Auntie, was it really a joy, your, um, marriage?"

Ella's face brightened, making her look years younger. "Oh heavens, yes. My Henry was very good to me. My one regret is that I could not give him a child before he was taken from me. He so wanted to fill this house."

The light left her face. Ella had been a long time without her husband, but she refused to marry again, insisting Mr. Maguire would one day return to her from the sea. Shanghaied men did sometimes come home, but most had done so long ago. It was another reason Ella would not leave this house.

Ella dabbed at her eyes with a lace-trimmed hankie kept tucked in her apron pocket.

They had to stay here.

Ella stroked her cheek. "But, of course, I have both of you. A blessing."

Many women would find it a burden to take in two poor relatives, especially when one of them was sightless. Kate felt the jab of guilt, as she always did when thinking about Phoebe's condition. Kate knew full well what awaited Phoebe if anything happened to her—the asylums. Between Kate and her aunt they had created a home for Phoebe. But it was a far cry from what Kate wanted for her sister.

She longed to send her sister to a proper school, where she could learn to do more than knit socks. She had even found one, the Perkins School for the Blind in Boston, Massachusetts. But they could not afford the tuition, let alone the expense of the passage to travel around Cape Horn.

Kate rose and hugged her aunt who seemed surprised but then patted her back.

"Thank you," said Kate, drawing back.

"Whatever for?"

"Loving us."

"Oh, that's not hard to do. And you know there is nothing I wouldn't do for you."

Kate felt the same. It was she who had agreed to be his.

Ella beamed. "If Mr. Pickett wants to court you, I say good for him."

Kate grasped Ella's hand and drew a breath, preparing to tell her the truth.

"Auntie, Mr. Pickett is not courting me. He has asked me to be his mistress."

She drew back. "What?"

"And I've agreed."

Her aunt gasped. "But why? Why would you agree to such a…" She stilled as her eyes grew round. A moment later, Ella burst into tears. "I forbid it."

"It's done."

It fell to Kate to comfort her, assuring and reassuring.

Sometime later the bell at the front entrance gave a resounding *ding-dong!*

That brought Kate to the door. The deliveryman had a small package for her. She signed for it and then tore open the brown paper. Inside was a large midnight-blue velvet box. Her heart jumped as she looked for a card but found none. The man must have ridden at breakneck speed to a jeweler to have this to her so quickly.

Ella came into the hallway as Kate flipped open the hinged lid revealing a necklace displayed on a creamy satin platform.

Ella gasped.

Kate stared down at the multistrands of gold filigree punctuated with seven delicate rosettes. Such a romantic piece took her breath away. She loved it on sight.

Kate snapped the lid closed and handed the box to Ella. "Take the most you can for it and bring it to the bank."

"But he most certainly will want to see you wear it."

"It's mine now, to do with as I like." Kate gripped her aunt's hands as she clutched the box. "Promise me."

"Yes, I will."

"I have to see about a wardrobe. I only have one day."

"One! Impossible."

"I fear so."

Kate went to one of the better establishments in the city. How ironic that she should again be standing on the platform waiting for the seamstresses to hem the skirts, when just two days ago she had been the one upon her knees.

She did not allow herself to smile. She knew that each one of the lovely confections would cost her dearly. And she also knew the gossip that would begin the instant she told them who would be paying the bill. It would not be hours before the entire city would know that Mr. Pickett had a paramour.

It took great effort for Kate to stand straight and keep

her chin up when it seemed the weight of the world was collapsing on her narrow shoulders.

One day, one night, and then she would be his.

Cole stood with Sam at the station platform. "I've got to hand it to you. You've wrangled up more investors than I could find in a month."

"'Cause I know where to look and it ain't in church." Sam never missed an opportunity to give Cole a dig about his turnabout. He'd lost his partner for the hours after sunset since his marriage, and Saturday nights were just not the same. "I'm telling you, those miners up at Dutch Flats will understand the advantages better even than the shopkeepers. Supplies will be cheaper and the transport of their gold much safer."

"You don't have to sell me."

"I tell you I talked to a citrus grower who thinks he'll be able to ship oranges all the way to New England before they rot?"

Cole looked doubtful. "Maybe." The conversation lulled as the engine chugged into the depot. The freight cars were followed by two private rail cars Sam had shipped around the Horn all the way from Pennsylvania. The engine's breaks squealed and steam hissed from beneath the massive wheels.

Cole took up the conversation. "I heard from Washington on the land grants. Now if we can get approval on those loans. Until then we need all the capital we can raise."

Sam looked about again but saw no sign of Kate. He knew the check he'd sent for expenses had been posted and that she'd been to three dress shops as instructed, because they'd sent runners to approve the large order. That didn't mean she wouldn't get cold feet. Something about her didn't ring true. She was hot one minute and cold the next, as if she didn't know her own mind.

"I think we can get congressional backing once we have the route mapped. Cartographers are already on board. I also hired some Pinkertons to ride along as guards. Head man's name is Allen Crawford."

"Pinkertons?" said Sam, straining his neck to see beneath the wide-brimmed hat of a woman approaching to his right. Damn he hated women's hats. Kept a man from running his hands through their hair.

"Just in case there's more trouble. Still don't know who's taking potshots at our workers, but I'd lay odds it's the stage owners or those shippers in Frisco."

Sam nodded. "Railroad would sink their business."

"I agree. Crawford is staying here to track down some leads. I gave him the names of the men in San Francisco who have shouted the loudest at the folly of a railroad. And he's spoken to the men who attacked you."

"You think they're connected?"

"Crawford does. They told him that they don't know who hired them. The woman was their contact. So he's trying to find her."

"All right, then."

"Did you hear a word I said?"

Sam scowled. "Crawford, Pinkertons and the woman knows the man responsible."

Cole laughed, but Sam didn't join him.

"What's wrong?"

Sam tugged his hat down. "I hope you know what you're doing, sending me back up there."

"You're the best man I know for this job. If you can organize that mill and the tunnel team the way you organized our mine, we'll be over those mountains in less than eighteen months."

Sam stared toward the east.

"It's mid-April, Sam. Even if it does snow, it can't last long."

Sam felt as cheerful as a pallbearer when he met Cole's eyes. "My head knows it, but my heart is jumping in my chest."

"I wondered why you were so antsy."

Sam stooped to glance under the bonnet of a passing woman.

"Sam, who the hell you looking for?"

"Kate Wells."

That stopped Cole. "The one from the alley?"

"She's coming with me."

Cole rolled his eyes. "Papers will eat that up."

"Like I care."

"You sure she didn't have anything to do with the robbery?"

"She didn't."

His quick denial raised Cole's eyebrows but Sam could not hide the fury the accusation raised. His need to protect her surprised him as much as Cole.

"Hope you know what you're doing."

Sam was looking at the mountains, but seeing the ghost he'd left behind.

"So do I."

Now Cole was scanning the area. "Crawford looked into her background."

Sam snapped his head around. "What?"

Sam's indignation lasted until his curiosity overwhelmed him.

"Well, after you asked me about her, I got curious."

"You're nosier than a woman, I swear."

"You want to hear what I got or not?"

Sam pressed his lips together, fearing what he would hear. He gave a quick jerk of his head.

"She was sixteen when she married Wells. Paraded all over with him. Lived like a queen, best of everything. He even took her up to the gold camps." Cole leveled his gaze on Sam.

The implication was clear. The miners would remember her and the association wouldn't be good.

"I've got a legitimate offer."

"You don't have to convince me."

But he did have to convince the miners.

"What do you know about Wells?"

"Her husband? Came out of nowhere. Scoundrel, cheat, peacock of a man. Liked to wear velvet coats and top hats. Terrible at cards, but a quick talker. Sold claims he never owned. It's a wonder he didn't take the money and run. Didn't seem stupid."

"Big, small, what?"

"Let's see. He was big. Solid, you know. Built a little like you. Same color hair. Wore a waxed mustache. Did I tell you he had a ruby stud in his tie this big?" Cole made a circle with his thumb and first finger to indicate the size.

Sam scowled. He didn't dress like a peacock, but it

was possible that he resembled her husband enough to give Kate second thoughts. "How'd he treat her?"

"Oh, like I said, best of everything. Lived in grand style. Fancy clothes, servants, the works."

Something wasn't right. Sam could offer her a similar arrangement, minus the marriage. Yet she shut him down before he could even make the offer. She meant it, too. He'd have laid a bet that she'd never change her mind. What *had* changed her mind? He shifted uneasily as he recalled Cole's implication that she might be involved in the incident in the alley.

No, he didn't believe it. Kate was the first good thing to happen to him since the railroad.

But he admitted that the passion that fired his blood scared her. He sensed it. She was like a seesaw in a school yard, flipping first this way and then that. But he'd given her no reason to fear him. And that left just one thing.

"Was she happy?" he asked.

"Why wouldn't she be?" asked Cole.

"Wells have any others before her?"

"Don't know." He met Cole's inquisitive eyes.

"Put your detective on that one."

"Sure. Soon as he finds out who's trying to kill you."

Sam refused to be drawn from his speculation. "I can't put my finger on it, but I'd swear she's scared."

"Of you? She's got more sense than I thought."

Sam growled at the sarcasm but kept to the point. "I'm gentle with my women. But she's skittish as a new mare. Something happened to her. I've seen horses like that, ruined by the wrong handling."

Cole laughed. "Sam, I've been married for nearly

twelve years. I don't know much. But I do know that if you ever compare that woman to a horse in front of her, you'll regret it forever."

Cole's laughter died alone and he stared at his friend. "All right, I'll bite. What's she scared of?"

"I think he mistreated her."

"Bastard."

"When she came to my place, she was sending all the signals of a woman with needs, but then she kinda froze up. She ain't a virgin so I'm just supposing that maybe her only experience was bad."

"Why would you want an unwilling woman?"

"She's not. There's a heat between us. I feel it. She does, too. I'm certain. She *is* willing, just uneasy." Sam scowled at the train before him, thinking how she had kissed him and then drawn back.

Cole stared at him. "Damn, Sam, I haven't seen that look on your face since you first hit that piddly little vein of gold and were bound and determined to follow it straight down into that mountain." Cole hesitated. They both were well aware how that hunch had turned out.

"I got to get her to trust me, is all."

Cole lifted an eyebrow in a skeptical expression that Sam knew well. "Might just be a ploy to get your attention."

"It's not," he snapped, and folded his arms across his chest. Why did he suddenly want to throttle his best friend?

Cole's eyes widened in surprise. "You're defending her? That's a first. Careful or she'll end up with a ring on that left finger."

Sam cast him a dark look. He wasn't sticking his head in that noose for anyone. The idea of raising a family scared him worse than winter in the mountains. But he kept that to himself because didn't want another sermon. His friend couldn't understand Sam's reluctance, but to explain it would mean telling him about his past and he wasn't going there for anybody.

Sam thought of what Kate had said about her independence. "If she intended to be a wife, I imagine she'd already be hitched."

Cole nodded his agreement. "I hear she's lovely, but any man that comes after Wells will have to deal with her reputation—and his. And a man rich as you, folks will just assume that's why she's with you."

"Let them think what they like and be damned."

Why was Cole smiling?

His partner had the wrong idea about Kate. She worked two jobs to make ends meet. If she was as mercenary as Cole painted her, why hadn't she found another protector already?

Waiting for another big fish, came the reply. His mood soured further.

He glanced at his watch. It was five after nine. Was she coming? He'd thought of nothing but her since he'd left her in the parlor. Kate's hands gripping his shoulders, her body pressed flush to his. Sam smiled and found Cole staring, his mouth in a sour twist.

Cole shook his head as if in pity. "You're falling hard."

"I just want to bed her."

"Keep telling yourself that, my friend. But something about this one feels different."

"Not so different."

Cole glanced over Sam's shoulder.

"That must be her."

Sam turned and, suddenly, he forgot how to breathe.

Chapter Seven

Sam's back was turned to her, but there was no mistaking him. His height and muscular frame would make him stand out anywhere. He was an unusual combination of muscle, neither gawky nor stocky, but a blend of elements that somehow made him more than the sum of his parts. Kate beckoned to the porter to indicate he should follow her with the handcart. Funny how easily she slipped back into the life she had abandoned over a year ago, only this time, Phoebe was safe at home, instead of locked up with a strict caretaker. Kate felt it her duty to look after Phoebe and that meant keeping their home. She straightened her shoulders and forced a smile.

The day was bright and the sunlight shone off the spring-green satin of the skirts of her elaborate day dress. She had chosen to wear the smaller, more flexible hoops today because of their practicality for sitting and entering smaller passages. But mainly she had chosen the dress to accent her eyes. The milliner had embellished the wide pleated pagoda sleeves and stiff, lace collar with an emerald-green velvet ribbon. Buttons, swathed in the same satin, ran up her fitted bodice in a neat, even row. She carried nothing but her new velvet reticule that matched the emerald velvet ribbon that ringed her sleeves and waist.

The man Sam spoke to nodded toward her and Sam turned. His mouth fell open as he gaped at her transformation. She smiled as she drew closer and noted how the tall, dark man beside him elbowed Sam in the ribs. Sam's mouth snapped shut.

"Here we are," she chirped, drawing to a halt before Sam.

She knew this part and played it effortlessly. She was to be beautiful, charming and vapid as weak tea. She was to have no opinion except his and accept Sam's will over hers. She forced down the urge to rebel as she leaned forward and kissed his cheek. When she drew back, he still stood gawking. It felt good to have him so off balance. She smiled sweetly and waited.

The porter grew impatient. "Where would you like these, sir?"

"Follow me," said the man who had elbowed Sam. He turned to Kate, extending his hand. "I'm Cole Ellis, the mute's business partner."

"A pleasure, Mr. Ellis. Will you be joining us up the mountain?"

"Not this time, I'm afraid." He tipped his hat and then addressed Sam. "I'll see her bags are placed in the private car."

Sam continued to stare at her.

Mr. Ellis slapped Sam across the shoulder with

enough force to send him staggering forward a step. The blow seemed to rouse him. Sam blinked.

"I said I'm putting her bags in the private car."

"Thanks," he said, but never took his attention from Kate. His eyes glowed with pleasure.

Her body reacted to his obvious approval, and she stepped closer. He gripped her cinched waist with both hands, taking possession of her. She did not like being captured but tried not to let his eagerness spoil the moment, for she was, in truth, happy to see him again and pleased at his reaction to her new apparel. It took a moment to become accustomed to his touch, but he did not yank at her or force her against him. Instead, he seemed to be holding her at arm's length in order to take her in.

"Hmm. You look good enough to eat."

Now the smile she held was genuine. He released her and she found that she missed his light touch.

He stepped closer. She stared up at him, suddenly light-headed. Was it the corset or the intensity of his stare?

Every time she got near the man she completely lost her head. And she knew better, if any woman alive did.

"Moth to the flame," she whispered.

He smiled. "You are a lovely flame."

She pressed her palm to her bosom. "*I'm* the moth."

His eyebrows lifted in surprise, then he grinned and slowly shook his head. "I don't think so." He leaned in. "I can't wait to have you alone."

Her eyes widened that he would say such a thing, right here on the platform. True, his words were just a whisper, but now she was blushing like a schoolgirl while Mr. Ellis directed the porter away. Perhaps this was the kind of thing one said to a mistress in public.

"Shame on you," she whispered back.

One hand slid to the small of her back as the other hand entwined their fingers, as if he meant to dance with her. He pressed her forward and suddenly she wished she had worn the larger hoops. A rush of excitement rippled through her and she stared up at him.

Shock stilled her as she realized she was full of anticipation. Her legs brushed together, bare of all but her sheer stockings and garter belts. She felt wicked and wanton, right here in the bold sunshine.

Mr. Ellis returned and had to clear his throat twice before Sam released her.

"Send word back if you need anything," he said, but his gaze flicked to Kate as if to say he didn't expect to hear a word. "And try to leave the train to speak to a few investors."

"I will," said Sam, his voice indicating he did not appreciate being nagged.

Mr. Ellis touched the brim of his black hat. "Nice to meet you, Mrs. Wells."

Sam released her long enough to shake hands with Mr. Ellis. Then he recaptured Kate, leading her to the railcar and assisting her up the steps.

She paused just inside as she noted for the first time that this was no ordinary passenger compartment, but a private suite. Her composure slipped as she took in the sumptuousness. There were no rows of padded seats or conductors waiting to see a ticket. The ceiling was painted a rich cranberry and etched in gold with a leaf motif. Thick velvet curtains in burgundy flanked the windows, their gold fringe and tassels an exact match of the five padded easy chairs. Toward the back, just before the bar, sat a full-size sofa also in gold damask. Carpets stretched from one wall to the other and a beveled mirror caught the sunlight and sent rainbows dancing on the ceiling. Beside the bar lay a narrow hallway behind which she assumed was the necessary.

Her breath caught at the opulence. It was so different than what she had expected. Luke had been outwardly flamboyant. To the world, he appeared vastly wealthy, but that was all part of the charade. He lived only by deception, which was why his private quarters, and the meager room he rented for Phoebe were stark in comparison to his outward extravagance. She had discovered after his death that some of her jewelry had only been rented.

But this was Sam's private quarters. No one would see this place but his closest friends and associates. Would his bedchamber be so elaborate?

"Do you like it?" he asked.

"Of course." She stepped into the room. "What keeps the chairs from toppling over?"

"Bolted to the floor."

That did make sense. Silence stretched between them as they faced each other. They would be completely alone on the trip to Dutch Flats.

"Something wrong?" asked Sam.

"Nothing," she lied. Of course a man as wealthy as Sam could rent a private car—or did he own it?

"You expected something else, Kate?"

"No, Sam, it is the loveliest coach I have ever seen."

She allowed him to lead her to a chair and was grateful he had not chosen the sofa. Her head was spinning with possibilities. But he did not set upon her like some beast, as she'd feared but instead knelt by her side.

"They're just loading up. We'll be departing soon. Would you like a drink?"

"Water?"

He went to the bar and poured her a glass, returning with a cut-crystal goblet. Kate's hand trembled as she reached for it, but once in possession of the narrow stem, she regained some control.

"My bags?"

"Through there." He indicated with a nod of his head. "Sleeping car."

Her hand began to shake so she tipped the goblet, taking several sips. Sam returned it to the bar, giving her a moment to regain her fleeting composure.

He moved with disturbing swiftness. When he returned, she had set her reticule aside and stood by the window.

Sam brushed his palm along her forearm, using it as a guide to reach her hand. His touch pitched her heart into a fast jig. She inhaled sharply at the sudden flash of heat blooming over her skin. He stood so close she could feel his heat, as well. His fingers caressed hers. She was thankful for the gloves that deadened the sensation, but not the quickening of her blood, racing through her.

"You look flushed," he said, seeming pleased at the success of his seduction.

She pressed a hand to her cheeks as she looked out at the platform to see Mr. Ellis staring at her through the window. She had the distinct impression that he was judging her.

Sam stood just behind her, reaching to close the blind

and blocking out her view. It would be so easy to lean back against his broad chest.

She turned toward him, fighting the need to press herself to him, to feel the gratifying pressure of his firm body against her soft curves.

His hand splayed across the center of her back, bringing her to him and granting her unspoken wish. She exhaled in a soft groan of pleasure.

She was supposed to be using her charms to toy with him, but all she could think of was how much she wanted to kiss him. Kate lifted her chin to ask him— what? His brown eyes held flecks of gold. His pupils dilated, pushing back the golden iris until it rimmed the dark center.

"Don't be afraid of me," he whispered.

How did he know?

Had he felt her heart as it hammered in her chest?

She wrapped her arms about his neck. He exhaled his relief and his shoulders sagged for just an instant. Then, he seemed galvanized to action. He drew her back from the windows, pressing her to the dark-paneled wall with his chest and dipping to kiss her.

His mouth slanted across hers at exactly the right angle. His tongue moistened her lips and she opened for him, allowing him to explore and tease and tempt.

As he deepened their kiss, she lifted up to her toes in an effort to be closer to him, tugging on his shoulders, demanding more. The deliciousness of his mouth made her yearn for him with a wildness she could not resist.

His hands moved in symphony, one cradling her head, as the other splayed across her back. He dipped to kiss her neck and her head fell back to give him access. His hand scaled over her stays to find the soft swell of her breast. He kneaded her yielding flesh, finding the hard nub of her nipple and rolling it, causing a shaft of almost painful delight to fire straight to her core.

"Oh, yes," she gasped.

His mouth trailed to her ear, licking and nibbling the soft shell and then sucking the lobe.

"You taste so sweet. I'll never get enough of you."

His hand moved from her breast and she moaned her discontentment at his abandonment.

A moment later she felt the heat of his palm, descending from her throat and into her chemise. She gasped as his bare hand cupped her naked breast, lifting and weighing her soft flesh. She bit her lip to keep from crying out her delight.

His mouth trailed down her neck, dropping burning embers of heat with each kiss. He was going to take her nipple into his mouth. She knew it and arched her back, offering herself to him.

His lips brushed her sensitive flesh and she groaned. He opened his mouth and drew her in, sucking on one breast as he fondled the other.

Never in her life had she felt this pulsing desire. It beat with her heart at the juncture of her thighs. She was frantic to have more. Nothing could stop them.

"Mr. Pickett?"

She stiffened.

Sam drew back, leaving her breast cold, wet and exposed. Before them stood a young man, dressed in the dark blue wool jacket of a conductor. He held a silver platter heaped with cheese, bread and a bowl of fresh sliced fruit.

"I have the light fare, as ordered, sir." He closed the door and turned, suddenly stupefied to the spot.

"Idiot." Sam's tone made the word sound like a dismissal.

The man glanced at Kate, as she tried to fasten her dress. How in the world had Sam disassembled her so quickly?

"I'm sorry, sir."

Sam's lips were now pinched tight and he glared, lifting an eyebrow as if cocking a pistol.

The young man started to creep backward as Sam stalked forward.

"Give me that," snapped Sam, relieving him of the tray. "Now git."

He did, bowing and then turning tail and running out the door and out of sight.

Sam called down the stairs. "Do that again and I'll shoot you."

Sam carried the tray to a small table before the couch and thumped it down.

The interruption presented Kate with the opportunity to think. Instantly, panic squeezed her throat. Somehow Sam's touch made her forget her fears. But without his arms about her, her courage fled.

He returned to her. She maintained her outward stillness while, inside, her heart raced as she struggled to breathe. She had reached the moment of reckoning. Sam was entitled to take his pleasure and she could do nothing to stop him.

She began to quake.

His gaze swept hungrily over her and without asking, he reached. She closed her eyes braced to be set upon.

She waited. Nothing happened. She opened one eye and found him glaring at her.

"Tarnation, woman, I'm not going to hurt you."

He grasped a carafe of wine from the bar behind the sofa and poured a glass. He thrust it at her.

"Drink it," he ordered.

She did, feeling the slight acrid burn of the tart burgundy liquid. It pitched in her stomach and she feared she would not keep it down. But after a few moments, a pleasant warmth filled her.

Sam sat beside her, waiting as she finished what he had poured. Perhaps he was right to offer spirits. Luke had often given her champagne. A small amount did take away some of the dread. She took careful sips until she had finished the wine.

"Better?" he asked.

She nodded and he took the empty glass.

"If you made a mistake, you best say so while there's still time to get off."

She found her tongue but could not meet his gaze. "I don't know what you mean."

He snorted. "I'm not so besotted with you, Kate, that I can't see it. No matter what our agreement, I'm not taking an unwilling woman."

Chapter Eight

Kate gasped in shock at his candor. His eyes narrowed in a silent challenge, daring her to deny it.

She deliberated her options—either tell him the truth or lie about her obvious reluctance, and she wasn't a good liar. Just the idea of speaking of her marriage bed to Sam made her cheeks flush. To reveal such a personal, embarrassing truth deflated her like a fallen cake.

He watched her like a cat that had cornered a mouse. She stared up at him and felt her eyes fill with tears.

"Oh, hell no." He rose. "I'm taking you home."

He stood and marched to the door.

"Foster!" he shouted.

"No!" Her word was too sharp and far too desperate.

He stared at her in shock, and then closed the door.

"Despite what you think of me, Mrs. Wells, I'm not the sort to make a woman weep." He stared at her now as if she were some strange and dangerous creature. The heat had left his gaze to be replaced by a tight-lipped control and guarded expression.

She pressed her gloved fist to her mouth, pinching her eyes shut against the humiliation of this moment. She could not look at him as she spoke the truth.

"It is not you, Mr. Pickett. It was my husband. You see, I didn't enjoy his attentions."

She felt the sofa sag under his weight as he sank down beside her, but could not seem to lift her chin off her chest to look at him.

"I knew it," he whispered.

Her astonishment momentarily surmounted her shame and she glanced at him. "You knew?"

"I suspected that from the way you freeze up on me whenever we get too…involved." Sam stroked her arm.

"He said there was something wrong with me."

"There isn't."

Her heart warmed at the speed with which Sam came to her defense.

"He hurt you?"

She nodded.

Sam clenched his jaw. His eyes narrowed to slits. As the blood rushed to his face, it fled hers. She stared at an expression so full of rage that she could not keep from cowering.

"That lousy, miserable bastard."

She winced at the cold fury of his eyes and glanced away, staring at the fringed window curtains. She had told no one the intimate details of her marriage, not even her aunt. She was too deeply humiliated by how she had been treated and, yet, Sam's reaction was not what she expected. He had been furious. That was true, but not with her. He was angry with Luke.

She glanced back, seeing the carefully contained wrath evident on his face. Even with the vein in his forehead throbbing with each beat of his heart, he did not shout at her. She'd never met a man who displayed such self-control.

God knows, Luke had none. He was like a child taking what he wanted and throwing a tantrum when denied. Kate squeezed her eyes shut, trying to banish the images of Luke's hands choking her as he pushed her legs apart.

Sam's voice dropped to an angry growl. "It's a good thing they hung the bastard or I'd be wanted for murder."

Her eyes rounded in shock. He was championing her? The warmth returned to her icy fingers and she smiled. Could Sam be any different than Luke?

His eyes remained trained on her, but his head was turned half away as if it hurt him to look at her.

"Why'd you marry him?"

She resisted the urge to squirm. "Foolishness. I was too naive to recognize the sort of man he was. My mother saw right through him, of course. He'd tried to come sparking, but she sent him off. She didn't think it proper for a man to stop a lady on the street.

Sam pressed his lips together. Did he recognize he had done much the same himself?

Kate filled the awkward pause with more talk. "I was so angry." Her chest constricted at her pang of regret, but she lifted her chin and met his steady gaze. "It's terrible to be able to see everything so clearly when you look back, isn't it? But at the same time he seemed so gallant…" She shrugged her shoulder. "Then my mother passed quite suddenly. Luke came to pay his respects."

Sam nodded.

Kate could not deny the fox had raided the henhouse the minute the hound was absent. Why hadn't she seen it?

"He came upon me at a hard time, quite desperate really. I didn't know what to do, who to turn to. Luke took care of everything. He saw to the flowers and the casket, even the service. He was like a white knight from some fairy tale." She glanced at Sam and found his jaw ticking.

"What about your aunt?" he asked. "Couldn't she help you?"

"I think she most certainly would have, had she known. You see, we were estranged. My father did not approve of her marrying a Catholic. She came as soon as she learned of my mother's passing from the list of victims in the paper. And she tried to visit, but I never knew. Luke sent her away without telling me." Kate laced her trembling fingers carefully on her lap and forced a smile. "As I said, I was foolish."

"He took advantage of you."

"Perhaps. But I am the one who married a man I hardly knew. I value my autonomy more highly now."

"And it's a good reason to be skittish of men." He rubbed his jaw. "That still leaves our current predicament."

She nodded. "Yes."

"I'll never mistreat you that way, Kate."

She wondered why she should believe him. Experience had taught her men did not always keep their promises. Still her instincts told her he was not a cruel man. But she had been wrong before.

There was a knock and Sam called his permission to

enter. Kate saw the top of someone's head. A face popped into view in the window of the compartment door, then disappeared again, like a gopher ducking back into his hole. The door cracked open and Kate could see only an arm.

"You called, sir?"

"Go away," said Sam.

"Yes, sir. The engineer says she's got a full head of steam and is ready if you are."

Sam looked at Kate. "Final call," he said.

She laid a hand on his forearm. "I'm staying with you."

He gave her the most winning of smiles and she could not help smiling herself. She realized that she liked Sam. He had a kindness in him that she never would have anticipated.

Sam called to the conductor. "Tell him to let her go."

"Right away, Mr. Pickett."

The door eased shut. A moment later the car gave a shudder. Kate glanced about in anticipation. She'd never ridden on a train.

"Sit tight now, we're about to move."

Kate gripped the armrest of the sofa.

The long sharp whistle blast made her jump. Next, the train jolted forward with such force that, had she been standing, she most certainly would have been thrown to the floor. Kate looked out the window and had the dizzying sensation that the world outside was moving, instead of the other way around.

The black smoke billowed past the windows until she could see nothing. She noticed that Sam was studying her.

"Something, isn't it?"

She nodded in excitement. "Oh, yes. Quite smooth once it is going."

The world reappeared as the smoke dissolved like a fog. Kate leaned forward to watch the city flash by in a blur. She had never moved so fast in her life. Very quickly the buildings gave way to the fruit orchards and wheat fields. Kate's delight caused her to inch forward so she perched on the very edge of her seat.

"It's like flying." She turned to find Sam's attention centered completely upon her.

He returned her smile, but his eyes were hungry again.

Kate gripped the seat, bracing for another battle with her uneasiness, but it did not come. Instead, she felt something that only happened with Sam, and back was the tingling awareness she had first experienced in that alley.

His hand sat casually between them. She unclasped her fingers and reached for him but then lost her nerve. When she glanced up, she found him still regarding her with a constancy of purpose. His stillness seemed a facade, designed to appear nonthreatening, as if he ever could.

"I enjoy kissing you, Sam. But I keep thinking of what comes next." Somehow she met his stare. "I'm afraid."

He sat far back on the sofa and patted his lap. "Come here, Kate."

She hesitated only a moment and then did as he bade her, inching closer until her thigh pressed to his. Beneath her the steel wheels turned, carrying her away from her family and sending a pleasant vibration through the soles of her leather slippers and the seat beneath them.

Sam reached around her waist and plucked her from

her place, as if she were a daisy, instead of a full-grown woman of nearly eighteen.

"Oh," she said as he nestled her between his splayed legs.

He eased her back so she rested against the solid mass of his torso as if it were the backrest of her favorite chair.

She rested her head against his shoulder and he tugged at the strings of her new emerald hat. She imagined the peacock feathers were likely hitting him in the eye. So she removed the pins that secured the hat in place and set it beside them on the couch.

He hummed his approval and pressed his mouth to her temple, brushing her with a tender kiss. Then he caressed her arms with light feathery strokes more gentle than she would have dreamed possible.

Her shoulders relaxed. If only he would just hold her, just give her his wonderful kisses and nothing more.

She closed her eyes, enjoying the low vibrations of the car rolling down the tracks and Sam's rhythmic touch.

His voice was soothing now, all traces of dissatisfaction gone from his deep, rumbling voice.

"It won't be like that for us. I'll be gentle and see to your needs."

Needs? What was he talking about? The only thing she had wanted was for him to kiss her neck while he petted her like a Persian kitten.

"Trust me, Kate. Let me show you how good we can be."

He had given her no reason to doubt him. Her wariness did not come from anything Sam had done. And she realized it was not fair to judge him on the actions of another man. But weren't all men alike in this way?

Honestly, she did not know.

He had been more than patient and his touch was gentle—so different than Luke's. But she shifted restlessly between his legs now, as she found it more and more difficult to remain still.

His lips brushed her neck, caressing the bare skin between her ear and the top of her lace collar. Heat seeped into her like tea into warm water. She shifted again.

"That's it. Nothing but pleasure, I swear."

She closed her eyes and pretended to believe him. Perhaps he believed it, as well. Perhaps the women in his past were wise enough to make him feel welcome. She should do that.

His mouth found the shell of her ear, nibbling along the sensitive flesh. She trembled and sighed, lost in the sensual bliss of his ministrations.

Sam wrapped an arm about her waist, forcing her to stillness with the pressure of his hand on her stomach. His fingers reached from her ribs to her nether regions. He did not grope or paw at her, but waited, as if for her to become accustomed to the intimacy of his touch.

The heat of his hand and the arousing scrape of his teeth on her neck forced a groan from her throat.

The sensual assault was like nothing she'd ever endured. Her breathing grew erratic. Her hips shifted of their own volition. Her mind filled with the desire to feel skin on skin. Her breasts felt the now-familiar ache and she arched against the desire, tightening her muscles and offering her throat to him.

He peeled back her gloves, leaving her palms naked for his kisses. His tongue swirled on the sensitive skin at her wrist and she gasped at the erotic sight and feel of him. He nibbled at her bare flesh and her breasts tingled with a need to be stroked. Who would have suspected that touching her arms could cause a reaction so far away?

And somehow he knew what he did to her, knew that she longed to have his hands fondle her breasts, even as he kissed her neck. He kneaded her sensitive flesh, stirring an aching heaviness. But instead of sweet relief, his strong hands only made the ache more acute. She arched into his hand like a cat and felt the low rumble of satisfaction in his chest.

One hand left her and she whimpered her disapproval.

He gathered her skirt, yard by yard, until his fingers brushed over her stockings, advancing steadily along her knee, reaching her garter and the terminus of her stockings to the point where her cotton bloomers should have been. His hand paused.

"You did as I asked," he murmured.

"Yes," she whispered, not really knowing why she had done it. It was wicked and scandalous—just the sort of thing a mistress might do.

She turned her head and he swept down to claim a kiss. His mouth slanted over hers, his lips firm and tender. She sighed and his tongue sought entrance to her mouth. She met his sensual assault with a counterattack of her own, thrilling at the reflexive tightening of his grip upon her. His tongue swept over hers as she burned beneath him. She could not get enough air now, even though her breathing was fast and hungry. Something was happening inside her, some coiling pressure, building toward something. She did not understand, but she wanted…more.

His hand stroked her inner thigh. His fingers were calloused and the rough texture on her smooth skin made her writhe against him.

He gave a growl as his hips rocked against her in a motion with which she was well acquainted. But instead of dampening her desire, his movement only made her squirm. The kiss ended as Sam gasped, pressing his forehead to her temple.

"Enchantress," he murmured, and reached the juncture of her legs.

His warm fingers brushed the sensitive skin of her bare inner thigh. She flinched.

"Shh," he whispered. "Trust me."

She did, even knowing all that would come, she sensed this man was different. This was Sam. He would not hurt her.

Kate relaxed against him.

"That's right, let me touch you. Ahh—so sweet. Feel how wet you are."

The calloused tips of his fingers brushed her cleft. She gasped, tensed, but held still and open for him.

"Oh, sweet Lord," he murmured.

His fingers now slid over her slick skin, the gliding friction bringing sparks of delight flaring within her. She gasped at the pleasure gleaned from so slight a movement. Her entire being seemed focused on this one small spot.

"That's it, let me love you."

Her eyes squeezed closed so she might more fully experience the tension rising within the center of her body.

His other hand toyed with her erect nipple, causing a sharp increase in her need. When had he undone her bodice?

She could no longer keep still. Her hips rose to meet his stroke and he slipped a finger into her passage. Her eyes flew open in surprise.

"Let me touch you, everywhere, I want to please you."

His words assured her as his hands explored, delving in a familiar tempo that brought no pain at all. On the contrary, the feel of him sliding in and out, as his thumb drew over the sensitive peak of flesh between her legs, was the most erotic experience of her life. She wanted him to do this, wanted more.

"Oh, yes," she whispered, and felt his shoulders relax.

His clever hand moved more quickly now as his mouth fixed to her neck.

"How I want to kiss you." His words fanned hot across the wet skin at her throat.

But he *was* kissing her. She lifted her chin to offer her mouth and he chuckled and then dropped his head to kiss her lips.

He drove his fingers into her until she could only feel the wonderful building tension. She strained forward, bucking against his fingers and forcing him more deeply into her passage. His other hand slid from her breast to steady her hips. And then something broke loose inside her.

She arched as the cry tore from her throat at the wave of bliss that exploded out from the place where he touched her, rippling through her middle and down her legs to curl her toes.

The pleasure rolled on and on like fingers on piano keys, cascading up the ivory, to a crescendo.

One moment her body was arched tight as the bow of a violin and the next she collapsed against him. He dropped her skirts and drew her back, rocking her as he rested his cheek upon the top of her head.

She wanted to thank him, to ask him what he had done to her, but all she could do was gasp for air. She could not even lift her arms to stroke his cheek. It was as if he had robbed her of all her strength. So she closed her eyes, floating in blissful relaxation unlike any in her experience.

She felt his lips press to the shell of her ear as he alternated kisses and whispered endearments.

Time drifted and all the while he held her close as the train car hummed beneath them.

At last her breathing slowed, her muscles recovered and she eased up. His arms tightened, as if he would not let her go just yet. But he relented and she straightened.

She glanced down at her skirts, still in disarray. Her legs lay exposed for all to see. She drew her hem down past her ankles.

She stared up at him, gaped really, taking no offense from his satisfied smile.

"Where did you learn to do *that?*" The instant the

question sprang from her lips, she regretted it and blushed furiously.

He laughed. "Well, a gentleman never tells, but I've never been one of those, so I'll just say that I've been blessed with some extraordinary teachers."

She could not repress the flash of jealousy and so veiled her eyes, wondering if it was fast enough to keep him from seeing her possessiveness. It was an emotion a mistress could never afford.

She had been with a man, and he seemed unruffled by it. So why should the thought of him doing this to some other woman fill her with violent intentions?

"I've never…" She didn't know where to begin.

He chuckled. "Something, isn't it? That's what a man can give a woman."

She already knew how a man found his pleasure, but she had never suspected she was capable of experiencing her own. Suddenly, she understood why her husband had been after her all the time. If he felt one-tenth the power of her fulfillment, it was understandable.

He took her hand. "It should never hurt you, Katherine, the loving."

She met his gaze, seeing the sincerity reflected in his eyes.

"If it did, then your man was a damned fool or a sadistic son of a bitch."

She cringed at his strong language and he clamped his lips shut. They had drifted into dangerous waters and so she steered them away from the shoals.

"May I have a little wine, please, Sam? My throat's gone dry."

She used his name, knowing he liked that.

He gave a half grin, as if he knew what she was up to, nodded and turned to the bar.

"Glad to," he said, his hungry eyes upon her again. "But we ain't done yet."

Chapter Nine

Kate clasped the delicate stem of the glass, casting glances at Sam. He had settled in one of the chairs across from her with his whiskey but, unlike Luke, he seemed more interested in spinning the amber liquid about in the fine crystal than drinking it.

Sam caught her eye and leaned forward, resting his elbows on his knees in a casual attitude. She had managed to button her bodice and replace her gloves when he was busy retrieving her beverage. But Sam had cast off his jacket, released his tie and unfastened the top two buttons of his shirt.

She looked out the window as she sipped her wine, avoiding the crackling tension building between them once more. What would it be like with Sam? She did not know but was certain it would be nothing like what she had suffered with her husband.

"Why'd you marry him?" asked Sam.

She looked him straight in the eye and said, "For the money."

Sam looked a little sick. "Did you love him?"

"No." She drew a breath to relieve the emotions that swirled like a dust storm inside her. "I did it to protect my sister. Perhaps it is impossible for a man like you to understand what one will do to survive."

His eyes narrowed and his jaw grew tight. He folded his arms across his chest and gave her such a look of condemnation she said no more. What had ever possessed her to tell him this much?

"I wasn't born with a bag of gold, you know?"

Kate gave a cautious nod.

"You might be surprised at what I understand about survival, Kate."

It was hard to imagine Sam in a situation he couldn't handle, one in which he was forced to do something that shamed him. She tried but failed. He was so strong, so confident. He met her silent regard and some of the stiffness eased from his shoulders.

"I'm sorry, Sam, if you suffered hardships. It was wrong of me to assume your life has been easy." She waited for him to elaborate, but instead he turned the conversation back upon her.

"So you'd lost your mother. What about your father?"

Her heart ached whenever she thought back to that hopeless time. She pressed her eyes shut for a moment and then met his steady gaze. "My father had died at sea when I was quite young. A little over a year ago, my mother got brain fever. They took her and I had to sell everything for her care. Luke helped me sell our house."

"I'll just bet he did."

"I didn't know then, what he did, about the fraud.

And so I married him. But not just for me. You see? For Phoebe. I was afraid they would take her to…" Her words trail off.

"And you didn't know your aunt?"

"I never met her until she attended my husband's funeral. Before that I was alone with my little sister. I had no money, no home."

"So, you sold yourself."

And she had just done so again for nearly identical reasons, but did not say it out loud.

He stared silently at her and she wondered if he was thinking the same thing.

"Your sister is lucky to have you."

More like cursed, Kate thought. Guilt gnawed at her like termites in fresh wood. From the outside she looked whole, but inside she was crumbling.

He pinned her with dark, mysterious eyes. Who was this stranger and what secrets did he keep buried in his heart?

He clasped her hand and brought it to his lips, kissing her gloved knuckles.

"I guess I understand why you've done it better than most. And I don't blame you."

He didn't? Why?

His thumb stroked the top of her hand. She laid her other hand on his, sandwiching it between her own. "Sam, do you have any family?"

"No longer. But I had a little brother, once."

Kate blinked in surprise. The way he said it made her certain something terrible had happened. His expression did not reassure. Why did such dreadful things happen to children—like Phoebe? What had happened to Sam's brother? She inched forward, unable to keep herself at a proper distance.

"Tell me," she whispered, bracing for whatever horror he might reveal.

"This 'cause you want to know or 'cause you want to buy some time?"

Kate had a clear conscience and so answered honestly. "I'd like to know something about you. It would make this easier for me if I felt I knew you a little."

"Believe me, Kate, you don't want to hear this." He rose and replaced his untouched whiskey on the bar, then returned to sit beside her on the sofa.

She stared him straight in the eye. "Now who is looking for a diversion?"

Sam couldn't help but smile at the cold conviction of her expression. The hellion from the alley had returned. He recalled the grit she had shown. He added that to the lengths she had gone to to keep her little sister safe and entertained the possibility that Kate might have the spine to hear this without pity or disgust.

"Things about my past are private. I don't want folks blabbing about my business."

A little line formed between her eyes as she frowned at this answer. "Earlier, you asked for my trust, a thing that must be earned. But I find that I do trust you, Sam. Are you willing to give what you have requested? Will you also trust me?"

"Your gender ain't known for keeping secrets."

"I think I might surprise you."

He gazed at her speculatively. "You already have."

"Have I?"

"First in the alley and now today. Never expected you to leave off those bloomers."

She smiled in a way that heated his blood. "All right, then."

Sam wished he hadn't set aside the whiskey. He wasn't ready to tell her that he and his brother likely had two different fathers or that each one of them was an unwelcome surprise. He couldn't say he was the son of a whore.

"He was five and I was twelve when my mom brought us to Our Lady of Sorrow." He didn't say that he'd tried to run away and his mother had brought him back to the nuns. "An orphanage in St. Louis."

Her eyes rounded and it was clear she feared the worse. He'd never spoken about Randy to anyone.

"She was sick. Spitting up blood."

Kate looked truly horrified so he hurried to tell her the rest.

"Told you, you won't want to hear it."

Kate swallowed. "But I do."

He pressed his lips tight and drew a lungful of air before continuing on. "Not long after that, they took him. A family wanted him. He was adopted, you see?"

She went pale. "They separated you?"

He dropped his head in shame—the one not chosen, the one left behind.

"They only wanted a little boy and I was half-grown."

Her voice was so earnest, so pure. "But to separate you, that was wrong."

He'd always thought so. It felt good to hear someone else say it. "Now you know me better than anyone, 'cause I never told that to a soul."

She graced him with a gentle smile that warmed him like sunshine.

"Have you tried to find him?" she asked.

Sam had and the rejection still cut deep. "He belongs to them now, to the other family that took him."

"But perhaps he wishes to know what became of you. He'd be so proud."

Sam's head lifted. "You think so?"

"Oh, yes. Look how well you've done. What is his name?"

"It's Randy, unless they changed it."

"You should find Randy, Sam. Make sure he is well and happy."

"Now you," he said, leaning forward, slightly anxious.

"Now me, what?" she asked.

"Tell me something you never told nobody else."

"I already have."

"'Bout your husband?"

She nodded, making a little humming sound of affirmation in her throat. "Not even my family knows how it was with me. I was too ashamed to tell them because it seemed my fault. I believed him, the things he said about me."

Sam wanted to take her now, prove that there was nothing wrong with her and that loving him could be a joy, instead of a burden. But he could see she was still reluctant. He sighed in the awkward silence.

"That dress is real pretty with your eyes."

She lowered them immediately, robbing him of the

lovely vivid green. "I'm glad you approve. I bought several different ones. Would you like to pick out what I wear or shall I?"

That flummoxed him. Had her husband… "Did he tell you what to wear?"

She kept her chin tucked to her chest and nodded.

"Then you pick. Definitely."

She smiled and peeked up at him. Was that approval he saw shining in her eyes? Suddenly that was more important than the burning desire he had for her.

"You hungry?"

She beamed at him and he felt the warm touch of gladness. He could wait. He'd be patient and let her get accustomed to him a little. Maybe give her pleasure again before he took his own.

He could see that they'd left the city and were climbing steadily into the narrow hills. They'd be in Dutch Flats in about two hours. What was he gonna do with her if he couldn't…

He got up and filled a plate of fruit and cheese. Get to know him, she had said. God help him.

Sam sat across from Kate in one of the lounge chairs. Between them was the tray of food. Cheese and bread, mostly, with some sliced ham and lots of fruit, peeled and cut into little bitty bites.

Kate didn't have much of an appetite, that was certain, though she did have an elegant way of eating that Sam appreciated. She set aside her gloves, for one thing, and he found her hands graceful as a bird in flight. He enjoyed watching her until she got to the fruit on her plate. Then the contentment faded and he started to think more steadily of bedding her.

"How old would he be now?" she asked, then daintily lifted a strawberry and brought it to her red lips, confirming that they were the same color. When he didn't answer, she paused, ripe strawberry speared on a fork, held just before her full lower lip.

What had she asked him again?

"Randy, I mean," she said.

Sam blinked, recalling himself. Maybe he'd best stare over her head. Damn, he was burning for her.

"Twenty-two."

"He might still need you."

He said nothing as his mood soured.

His plan to stare over her head failed as he could not keep his eyes off her. The strawberry disappeared behind strong, white teeth.

"Having a family is such a precious gift," she said.

This was exactly why he didn't generally talk to women. They had crazy ideas, like family being a gift. "A curse you mean. You should know. You lost most of yours, too." He sat back looking at her hair, which was reflected in the mirror behind the sofa. How many pins were there holding up that mass of auburn? How long was it? He already knew how it smelled, but was itching to see it shimmering down her back.

"I have my aunt and my sister. And they mean the world to me."

"I used to think like you—that the most important thing was to keep us together, just like you're trying to do now."

She seemed surprised by this comment. Did she

think he didn't know why she'd changed her mind? Kate hadn't been with a man in a year and then slammed the door in his face. He wasn't vain enough to believe she'd just suddenly fallen for him. She appeared to be a practical woman, despite her beauty, or perhaps because of it.

Sam continued. "Staying together ain't what's most important. In the end you do what's best for them." He wanted to make her understand. "Best for *them,* you see? Not for yourself."

"But staying together *is* what's best."

Sam snorted. "Randy don't want to see me." He stood and headed for the bar, determined to recover his glass of whiskey. He'd made a play at acting with civility. It pinched more than this damn banded collar of his new shirt. But if he was going to talk about Randy, he could at least have this small comfort. But halfway there he smelled lavender and changed direction, sitting beside her on the couch. What would she do if he tried to feed her those morsels? He wanted to. He'd already picked out the best from the platter for her.

She faced him. "How could you know that? He might be longing for news of you."

He couldn't keep the pain from showing and he could tell by the widening of her eyes that she noted it. He glanced to the window and watched tall ponderosa pines fly by in a blur. "I know because I did find him, after I figured out where the records were kept and how to get the keys. We'd been apart more than a year when I ran away from the orphanage. Hardly recognized him. He'd gained weight and was wearing fancy clothes. But he recognized me right off."

"Where did you find him?"

"Leaving his school, nice white schoolhouse with green shutters and a play yard with a teeter-totter and a rope swing. He spotted me and his eyes got real big. But instead of running to me, like I pictured, he started backing up like you do when you suddenly come upon a big, mean dog."

"Perhaps he didn't know you."

"I told him who I was. I called him by name, but he just kept scooting away." Sam's eyelids now became a damn, holding back a rising river of water.

Kate set her plate aside and rested a bare hand on his knee. His shoulders hunched.

"What, Sam?"

"He told me to go back where I come from, like I was some stray dog trying to follow him home. Finally, I had to grab him. Do you know what he did?" The damn broke and Sam turned aside to dash away the hot tears. His voice changed, growing strained. "He started yelling."

Her small hand squeezed his knee. "Oh, Sam, how terrible. What did you do?"

He kept his gaze on the window, but he didn't really see the landscape flashing by. Instead, he saw a narrow road in a small town on a big river, far away and long ago. "I just let go and he ran away. I followed him and he kept looking back. He lived in a big clapboard house with a yellow barn and geese that swam in a pond beside the milk house. He had a brown dog with a litter of little pups and he had a mom and dad.

"His mom had dark hair and she met him on the porch. She put an arm on his shoulder and then sort of steered him inside. She never saw me."

Kate rubbed his back, suddenly understanding why he never stayed with any woman for long. Why he never settled down like other men in his position. He wasn't willing to take the chance on losing anyone else. But none of that was his fault. Unlike her, he was blameless. She grimaced. "I'm sorry, Sam. I'm so sorry they didn't take you, too."

"It was a real big house. When the nuns said they didn't have room for me, I figured they lived over a store. I told them that I'd sleep by the stove. I was just a dumb kid. I didn't understand." He swiped his cheek again and then wiped his hand on his pant leg. "They had room. They just didn't want a foulmouthed ruffian who was raised by…"

She glanced at him. His head hung in shame. She assumed the worse.

Kate rested her head on his shoulder. "Did you go back to the orphanage?"

"No. I never did. I took one of the pups and set off on my own. But the dog was too young to be away from its mom and it died. I never should have taken it."

They sat in silence for a while, Kate rhythmically stroking his arm and the low rumble of the train filling the void.

"I thought he'd want to come with me—that he'd be waiting, that he needed me, like your sister needs you. But he was afraid he'd lose his new family. So I let him go."

"Would you have wanted him to go with you?"

Sam shook his head. "He was better off. It's what I meant about doing what's best for them."

"But now you must find him. He'll be wondering about you, carrying a burden of guilt for sending you away. That's a millstone no child should carry. And only you can relieve him of it."

"You think he'd want to see me after all this time?"

"Oh, Sam, I know it. You're so lucky, because you can still make this right, you still have a chance." She thought of her own millstone, the one she could never put down.

She felt her eyes grow hot. He lifted her chin with one finger. "You crying?"

"I lost someone, too—my baby sister. But she is gone forever because of me." There, she had said it aloud. The secret shame she carried each day had been spoken.

"What?"

She drew away from him, sitting stiff and brittle as an unfired pot.

"Her name was Rose. She was six months old and had just learned to crawl."

She glanced at Sam, but he said nothing, just sat waiting. Her voice became a low whisper as if this secret could not be spoken aloud.

"I got sick first, just a little fever, nothing really. My mom got it next and then the baby." Kate could barely speak now, past the tears choking her. "It was diphtheria. I gave it to them, all of them. It killed the baby and…" Kate pressed a hand to her forehead as the guilt bubbled up again to consume her. "Phoebe lost her sight." She looked at Sam, exposed and raw with grief. "And it's my fault, Sam, all of it."

Sam gathered her up in his arms. "Oh, no."

He pressed his lips to her forehead and rocked her as she clung to him like ivy on a garden wall.

"It's not, Katie."

But it was. She knew it. That's why she had never spoken of her guilt before. Not even to her mother. She knew she would have said something just like this. But it didn't make it better. The remorse still chewed at her. How did one make amends for such at terrible wrong? The answer came to her as it always did. She couldn't— not ever.

"Do you know what this means?" asked Sam. "We're the same inside. I couldn't keep my family any more than you could keep yours. But you, at least, managed to save a part of it, your sister and aunt."

The part she hadn't killed.

He halted the rhythmic stroking and took in her tear-stained face.

"I never spoke of this to anyone before and I never thought to meet anyone who could understand. But I think you do, because you lived it. Maybe it wasn't chance that brought us together in that alley, but something bigger."

He brushed the tears from her cheeks and she closed her eyes against the earnest, tender expression in his eyes.

His voice was soothing as a balm. "We've both got scars, both lost people we loved." Sam lifted her chin and she opened her eyes. "So we did things different than most folks." He stroked her cheek.

The engine vibrations changed, and Kate noted that they were slowing down.

"Getting close," said Sam. "I can't wait to see what

the miners think of you. I sent word ahead to the camps that I'm throwing a party to introduce them to the Union Pacific. Music, dancing, food and free beer. Should be a wild time."

Kate swallowed back her dread.

For a little while she had felt so attuned to Sam that she had nearly forgotten. But now it came crashing back. He intended to use her, just as her husband had done. Nothing had changed between them.

Chapter Ten

When they arrived in Dutch Flats, Kate was pleasantly surprised to see proper warehouses near the tracks and a grid of streets that stretched back five deep. Some of the buildings rose three stories tall and she counted two church steeples. She could hardly believe this was the rough jumble of canvas and mud she recalled.

The train slowed at a new train platform and small depot. Somehow an actual town had sprung up amid the tailing piles.

A crowd had gathered to greet them. Among the waving miners, Kate was thankful to see many properly dressed women.

"Your jaws are flapping open like a trapdoor, Kate. Just what were you expecting?"

"I thought it would be more…rustic."

"Not anymore. It's a proper town. I rented the Gold Dust for the shindig. You go change into a fancy dress and put on that necklace I gave you."

Kate's stomach gave a lurch.

"It's okay. I'll be waiting right outside. All your things are in the next car."

He left her pale and shaken. Kate hurried to the sleeping compartment but paused upon entering, overwhelmed by the opulence. The bed was large and magnificent with a carved headboard and half canopy draped with velvet curtains. She went to the cherry armoire, opened it and found all her new dresses displayed on wooden hangers without so much as a wrinkle in any of them. She selected the royal-blue satin with the pearl trim.

She unbuttoned her dress and carefully hung it with the others. Then she drew on her bloomers and exchanged the small flexible hoop skirt for the wide stiff set. By the time she had burrowed into the new gown, she recognized two things. One, she would have to fix her hair herself and, two, she could not possibly fasten the back of the dress alone.

Many minutes later she emerged from the car, red faced and panting, with a lace shawl about her shoulders and her hair in some semblance of order.

Sam had finished greeting the men and had sent them off to the saloon.

She stood on the steps of the compartment until he turned to notice her. He stopped in midsentence to stare. She found his look of astonishment both flattering and somewhat irritating. Had she looked so shabby in her new green day dress?

He walked away from the two bearded men without a word and then extended his hands to lift her down. She leaned away.

"I can't come out," she whispered from behind her fan.

He dropped his hands. "Why not?

"You promised me servants. Had I known I would be dressing myself I would have chosen a far different wardrobe."

He looked thoroughly confused.

"My dress is not fastened!"

He grinned. "Little overanxious, ain't you?"

She batted him with the folded fan. "Don't you dare make jokes. This is a desperate situation. I need help. And since there is no lady's maid to assist me…"

"Always glad to help a lady."

She backed up the steps, awkwardly, managing not to tread on her hem. Once inside she lowered her shawl, revealing the row of tiny buttons to him.

"Holy crow. There must be a hundred of them."

"Please, Sam."

He lifted his hands to the bottom of the row just at her hips and she felt a slight pull, followed by a chuckle.

"Never buttoned one up before."

She gasped. "Stop that, you dreadful man. A gentleman would never say such a thing to a lady."

"Yeah, but this is just us talking."

She could not keep from smiling at this and was grateful he could not see it. He worked diligently for several minutes as she held her breath to assist him.

"Uh-oh," he said.

She looked back at him over her shoulder.

"Misaligned. Have to start again."

Her shoulders drooped and he laughed. The next moment his warm mouth was pressing to the bare skin at her neck. She spun in his arms and he gripped her waist, staring down at her with warm brown eyes.

He looked different, happy perhaps. This was something new, an expression she had not seen before. She liked his gentle teasing.

"Looking forward to doing this again, in reverse, later on."

She cocked her head and decided to try her hand at teasing him. "Well, I'll have you know I am wearing bloomers for the occasion."

"That shouldn't slow us down much."

She felt herself actually looking forward to it. She blinked in utter astonishment. When had her feelings toward these intimate deals changed? She glanced at Sam, quite flabbergasted at her realization. He said he would never mistreat her and that had been all she had hoped for. Yet, in fact, he had given her so much more. Anticipation curled inside her and she glanced at the bed.

He grabbed her hand. "Oh no, you don't. I got half the town waiting to meet you and hear why they can't live another day without owning a piece of that railroad."

She smiled as he drew her out of the coach and carefully saw her safely down the steps, before lifting her over the gap between the bottom stair and the platform.

He escorted her through the depot, the single ticket window now closed for the night. They emerged on the opposite side and she had her first close look at the town's transformation. She stared down a wide dirt street, lined with eateries and saloons. Their followers stood waiting and continued along, giving the town an atmosphere of celebration. The road ran only a hundred yards before dead-ending into another, wider street. The setting sun poured down the wide thoroughfare between the buildings, illuminating everything with a golden glow.

"That's Main down there. Hotels, the claims office and banks. Lots of shops, of course. Easy to bring goods in now with the railroad. Cheap, too. But there'd be no need if the claims weren't producing. Miners started it all."

"I believe the gold started it."

He smiled. "That's so. I still have a claim up here, though it never produced much. The saloon is just past the Black Bear Restaurant." Sam pointed and she turned her attention to the large two story clapboard that dominated the row of buildings. "Shall we walk?"

The street was dry, so she nodded her consent and they set off, arm in arm.

They reached the Gold Dust Saloon to find a large crowd already milling about. Sam stepped in and the group parted like the Red Sea. Kate had never seen anything like it. Men stepped out of his way as he passed, instinctively yielding to Sam. The room grew quiet as folks watched with singular fascination. Of course, Sam would be a hero here. The man whose claim paid out, the success story they all fought for. Their upturned faces glowed with admiration. But it was more than that. Sam was an unusual combination of mass and inertia that made him look more like a bounty hunter than the owner of the richest mine in California. He had a dangerous edge. She'd sensed it instantly and had been as wary as these people. But now that hard edge made Kate feel safe, as if no man would dare try anything with Sam as her protector. She smiled with new confidence as he escorted her to the bar and then recalled how unreasonably jealous Luke had become when men admired her.

Her smile vanished. Why dress her up in such finery if not to draw the attention of other men? Would he expect her to flirt and fawn, as Luke had and later make her pay for it? She had once been in a similar situation, one in which she could not win. And now, it seemed, fate had brought her to the same place again. Suddenly her stomach hurt.

Sam was tall enough not to need a platform to be seen over the heads of the others. She, on the other hand, was quite swallowed up in the gathering. Sam called for a chair and lifted her to stand on the seat. It was unnecessary, as he already had the attention of every man in the room. Kate's anxiety grew as Sam began his speech.

He was funny, at first, getting the crowd to laugh, and then he turned eloquent as he continued, speaking of the importance of commerce and trade and the safety and reliability of the railroad. He told the miners that the price of goods would drop dramatically if they could be shipped from the East Overland, instead of by steamer and then mule train. He told them that owning a piece of the railroad was owning a piece of history that would be more valuable than gold. Their sweethearts and family would not be more than a two-week ride from their claims and the rail cars would include parlors, where customers could gather to sing and play cards, and sleeper cars with bunks to sleep on at night.

Kate watched him, comparing him to Luke. Her departed husband had been a master at persuasion and he had been artful at closing a deal. But he worked with only three or four men at a time and he had never spoken with the passion Sam expressed. Plus, what Sam said might actually be true, which was never the case with Luke.

Kate listened, spellbound, as he spoke of the wagons struggling to cross through the passes, beaten by snow and at the mercy of the mountains. Something in his voice changed and the room became silent.

Kate wondered if she had misjudged him. Perhaps this was not about money and power, but something more important. No one laughed now or smiled. All the men in the room were caught in the moment, drawn by the force of Sam's words. When he told them it was the duty of every citizen of California to close that pass to wagons, they believed him. When he finished, there was a moment's silence, then the room erupted in a roar of approval.

Sam turned to the bartender and ordered two glasses of champagne. He lifted one, offering it to Kate.

"Make a toast, Kate," he whispered.

She lifted the glass high above her head.

"To the new shareholders of the Union Pacific Railroad," she called.

Men cheered and stomped their feet.

"If you'd like to be the first to own a piece of this fine venture, my clerk is sitting right by the windows. We'll accept coin, paper or gold dust. Free drinks to every stockholder in the room."

Cheers followed and then shouts as men struggled for their place in line.

Sam lifted Kate down. "Now drink up that champagne and get over there to sit with my clerk. See what you can do to encourage men to buy."

She felt a little deflated. The speech had made her feel patriotic and misty inside. But now the cold reality swept back in. She was here to persuade the miners. It was a role Luke had taught her well. She hated Sam for making her do it again, no matter how grand the cause.

He lifted her gloved hand to his lips and kissed the back of her hand. Then he smiled. The smile faded as he glanced at her bare neck.

"You forgot the necklace."

Kate tried to keep her eyes from widening. "Well, you rushed me out of there." She recalled Luke's wrath when he caught her trying to steel "his" jewelry and felt her stomach clench.

His smile returned.

She found she could breathe again. He didn't know. Not yet, anyway. But what would he do when he discovered the truth? She pressed down the urge to tell him. Her family needed the money and she still did not know Sam well enough to trust him. Kate retreated to the table and sat beside his clerk.

The shares were snapped up and the beer and whiskey flowed as dinner was served to all the new shareholders. Kate and Sam sat at the head of the gathering. Kate ate little, knowing that her corset would not permit her to fill her belly. After the meal, there was dancing. Kate was worried that Sam would encourage her to dance with the men. Quite the opposite was true. He was possessive and did not allow her to dance with anyone but him, curtly turning away all those who tried.

"I have never been the jealous sort before," he said as he led her to the center of the room. "Or maybe I just never had nothing to be jealous of."

She smiled at the flattery and then looked up to find complete sincerity in his eyes. She had grown accustomed to pretty words from Luke but now wondered if Sam's compliments were as heartfelt as they appeared.

She decided to believe him. "That is a very sweet thing to say."

He grinned and gathered her up in his arms as the fiddler began a rousing two-step. Sam swept her around the room as the others moved aside to watch them pass. Men clapped to the beat as Kate's feet flew beneath her voluminous skirts. When the music stopped, Kate was flushed and breathless.

"You're as pretty as a rosebud," he said. "It's why I gave you those roses."

What roses, she wondered and then recalled the ring of gold rosettes on the necklace. She would have to tell him that she had left the necklace safely at home and hope he was not too angry. But when she opened her mouth she could not get the words out.

"Might we stop for a drink?"

"Wine, whiskey or sarsaparilla?"

"I should think a nice glass of iced tea."

"I don't recommend water that ain't boiled. How about a beer."

"I don't drink beer."

"It's safer and it'll cool your thirst." Before she could refuse he placed the mug in her hand.

The smell reminded her of rising bread. She took a sip

and winced at the bitter taste. Had she not been so thirsty, she never could have swallowed it. Still, there was a bubble to it that was pleasant and it did cool her throat.

"You got a mustache," he said and then wiped her upper lip. He gazed at her. "Damn, I can't wait to get you alone."

Her smile faltered. He wouldn't abuse her. She knew him well enough to believe that. And he had not been drinking heavily. Sam waited for her to finish most of her beer before saying good-night.

No one seemed surprised that Sam was retiring early and there was much leering and backslapping as he escorted Kate out.

"Party will be getting wild now anyways," he said. "Best we get you home."

Home. She liked the way he said it, as if they had a home, as if they were not strangers about to share the most intimate of acts. She half wished they were not strangers, but lovers and friends and that she could rely on him to protect her instead of using her.

The cold reality was so much harder to take. But she accepted her lot, taking his offered arm and allowing him to lead her out into the night.

It had rained while they were inside and the road was now muddy. Sam stopped, and turned to the east.

"Be snowing farther up," he said and then he shivered as if the cold could reach him even here.

Kate lifted her skirts, preparing to ruin a perfectly lovely pair of satin slippers that had been dyed to match her gown.

"It seems a shame," she whispered.

"What?"

"To ruin the new slippers."

Sam glanced down at her hoops as if he could see her slippers through the curtain of fabric. "I could carry you."

"In hoops. I should say not."

"Well, take them off, then."

"What?"

"When I used to ford a stream, I'd just take off my socks and boots and carry them across. Keep 'em dry."

"But my feet will get muddy."

"Bet they'll wash better than the shoes."

"What about my stockings?"

He wiggled his eyebrows. "I'll help."

He was on his knees before her. Kate noticed they were drawing a crowd.

"No. It's all right. I'll just muddle through."

"Nonsense."

"Sam," she whispered. "Everyone will see my ankles."

"Let them."

Men laughed. He was making a spectacle of her. She flushed in shame.

"Give me your foot."

She did, resting a hand on his shoulder to steady herself as he pulled off her slipper and then located her garter as if he were a terrier down a rabbit hole. A moment later the ribbon was untied and the stocking and garter removed.

Her pale foot gleamed in the moonlight. "Kinda tiny," said Sam, then reached for the other and repeated the operation.

Then he threw her stockings over his shoulder and stood.

"Are you certain?" Kate asked.

"Let her go," he called.

Kate lifted her skirts high, giving spectators a clear view of her ankles and calves. The men cheered.

If he didn't care who saw, why should she? The shame vanished as she stood there, feeling suddenly free of constraint. They knew what she was and so did she. What was the point in pretending?

She stepped off the wooden walkway into the cold, squishy mud.

They walked along until they reached the depot, Kate leaving muddy footprints beside Sam's boot tracks. They passed the Pinkertons. The few men who had followed halted at the depot platform, allowing them to continue alone.

Once up the steps, Sam dragged off his boots, leaving them just inside the door. Then he scooped her in his arms and carried her into the coach, setting her gently on an upholstered chair. Kate kept her feet up and off the carpet.

"I'll get a basin." He left her and returned a few moments later with a bowl of warm water and a clean white towel.

The sensation of having him wash her feet was one of the most pleasurable experiences of her life. He soaped and lathered and rinsed and then rubbed them with the soft towel leaving no hint of soil.

"You would make an excellent mother," said Kate.

That made him laugh. Then the smile faded. "I used to take care of Randy."

She gave him a commiserating look. "I still take care

of Phoebe. I wonder if my aunt will help her wash her hair this Saturday?"

"I've interrupted your life," he said.

"You have."

"Will you forgive me?"

"That remains to be seen."

This caused his expression to turn devilish. Her breath caught as she realized she had inadvertently issued a challenge. And men like Sam lived for such contests.

Chapter Eleven

Sam stood and offered his hand. She had the urge to tuck her own under her skirts. But such childishness would not prevent him from taking his due. All she could hope was that he was a man of his word and that he would not use her too harshly.

She gave him her gloved hand and he drew her up to stand before him.

"Did you enjoy yourself this evening?"

"I can say I have never had an evening like it."

He laughed. "Not a hearty affirmation. You dance real well."

"As do you."

"And you were a help tonight. We sold more shares than I had expected."

"That was due to your speech, not my ornamentation. You were very eloquent. Passionate, even."

He looked astonished. "Was I?"

"Oh yes, especially when you spoke about closing

Broadner Pass and the wagon trains. The miners were so quiet that you could have heard a mouse scuttle across the far side of the room. It was as if you understood the suffering of the immigrants."

Sam went silent as he frowned. Now she recalled her earlier impression. A possibility raised its head and she could not keep from a sharp inhalation of air.

"Sam?"

"They were quiet 'cause they know I was a member of that party."

"What party?" But even as she said it she knew. "Oh, Sam, not the Broadner Party."

He gave a curt nod.

She covered her mouth with her hand as she tried to regain her flagging composure. Everyone new the story of the doomed wagon train that had arrived at the pass one day too late. Early snows had trapped them, food had run short. The bitter cold and heavy snows had blanketed the outfit like a shroud. Many had perished. Some said those were the lucky ones. Her eyes widened as she tried to fathom the implications of this revelation. Then she lifted her chin and stared up at him, smiling gently. She rested her fingers ever so lightly on his chest. It felt strange, awkward, but she did it.

"Well, no wonder you want to close that pass."

He nodded. "I want to do that more than anything on this earth."

"Well, *I* would not lay odds against you."

His expression changed again. The tightness around his mouth eased and his eyes turned warm and inviting. He captivated her into speechlessness.

"Will you allow me to help you with your gown?"

Her breath caught, but she nodded. He motioned toward the back of the car. She knew the sleeper coach waited just beyond. On bare feet she padded before him, feeling the thick woolen carpet beneath her.

He opened the door and then assisted her between the cars. She gasped at the cold metal of the platform beneath her feet. Then he held the other door and they were safely inside. The lock clicked behind her.

Kate inched away. She wanted to trust him and believe he would be gentle, but instead she found herself praying silently for deliverance.

It was one thing to lift her skirts for him to touch her, quite another to allow him to crawl under them.

Trust him.

Don't trust him. He's a man and a bloody big one.

Who has never raised a hand to you.

Don't give him the chance.

Her movements were cautious, and she slipped farther from him as if trying to escape a large wolf without drawing his notice. Sam followed her, his hopeful expression turning to concern.

Kate wrung her hands. Sam reached, she shied.

"What's wrong?" asked Sam.

"I... Nothing. Everything is fine."

Sam cocked his head for a moment and his brow descended over his eyes. "You're not much of a liar."

She pressed her lips together, damned if she'd mention her husband to this man again, although it was as if he stood here in the room with her. They were not the same, Sam and Luke. She knew it in her heart. Didn't she?

Sam's eyes widened and he seemed to notice how she trembled: "I'm not like him, Kate."

"I know that."

"Do you?" His eyes pinned her. "Then why has all the color gone out of your face?"

It seemed as if the blood had drained from her skin entirely and pooled in her belly. She liked Sam, but wondered how long until he destroyed her trust? She stared at his fists clenched at his sides. As she watched, he slowly released the corded knot of bone and muscle.

"I want this to be different from the others I've known, Kate. And different from what you've known, too, because…" He lifted a hand to her face and she turned away. His hand dropped.

"You don't understand," she whispered.

"I'm trying to." He lifted her chin and she knew what came next.

Her breathing stopped as his mouth descended taking her in a passionate kiss. She melted against him, all fear and uncertainty drowned in the warm, seductive waters of need. She looped her arms about his neck and pulled.

He stepped back, his eyes narrowing. "Mixed signals. What do you really want, Kate?"

She shook her head. "I don't know anymore."

Sam dragged her arms from his neck, putting several feet between them.

"You best decide before we go any further."

He released her, leaving her wet and wanting. Then he stepped away and walked out the door. She almost followed him.

Almost.

* * *

Clearly, Sam had lost his damned mind. It was the only explanation for his stupidity. That's what comes from breaking his own rule and paying for the company of a female.

What the devil had gotten into him, trying to take an unwilling woman?

But she wasn't always afraid of him. Sam knew how he could get her past her resistance and he'd nearly done it. He gazed at the door that led to the sleeper compartment, just one car away from the parlor coach.

He had never wanted a woman as much as he wanted Kate Wells beneath him. He wanted to rub his scent all over her and breathe deep of the fresh fragrance of her skin as he claimed her as his own. But instead of taking what he wanted he was curled on this velvet-covered horsehair sofa.

Madness or something worse.

It was a blow to his pride to see her hesitate. He wanted her to need him as much as he needed her. But she was still afraid, so he'd walked away.

Damn Luke Wells and may he burn in hell for what he had done to her!

He closed his eyes, recalling how she had melted all over him when he touched her. Her body knew its match, even if her mind resisted. He had to figure out how to convince her. He wouldn't take her otherwise. How he wanted her to come to him.

He snorted. As if that would happen. Likely she'd already bolted the compartment door. Not that this would stop him. He pictured himself kicking in the door.

"Oh, yeah. That'll do a world of good."

He could go into the camps. There were plenty of whores up here. That thought made his stomach sour. He threw himself onto his back. She had ruined him for other women. If he could just have her once, he might get past his obsession.

He heard the click of the door opening and reached for his pistol. After all the trouble at the camps and the attack in the alley, he wasn't taking any chances.

He rolled off the sofa and hunkered under the window, well out of the beams of moonlight that streamed into the coach. The intruder had taken off his boots and stepped as lightly as a cat. Another moment and he'd be in the light.

Sam raised his pistol but didn't cock it, knowing the sound would give away his position. Instead he pressed his finger to the trigger.

Kate stepped into the moonlight, her white ruffled robe fluttering about her like angel wings. How had she gotten those buttons loose by herself? He stared in wonder as she floated into the center of the room. His prayer was answered.

Kate had come to him.

At the beauty of her, the breath whooshed out of him. That mane of hair he had speculated on now flowed about her back in a river of dark waves, tumbling to her waist. Her tiny feet were bare and her skin was silver as the moonlight.

"Sam?"

He rose to his feet and holstered his gun.

"Here."

* * *

Sam moved within the ring of moonlight.

Kate stared into his haunting eyes. His hair was mussed and his chin was covered with a day's growth of whiskers, making him look dangerous and uncivilized. He had removed his coat and wore a white shirt, but not one button was fastened. The sight of hard flesh made her want to turn tail and run. But it also made her itch to stroke him. She listened to that deeper impulse and stepped forward.

His eyes flashed hungrily, but his expression remained tense and, she thought, melancholy. Sam reached and then hesitated, letting his arm drop back to his side, waiting, it seemed, for her.

Kate cleared her throat, hoping her voice would not fail her again. "I came to…to ask you… Sam, why didn't you…"

"Take what I wanted? Force myself on you? I'm hot as forge iron for you, but I'm not a monster."

She threaded her fingers together before her and met his gaze, wondering if she saw the spark of hope gleam there.

He remained where he was, his eyes glittering in the moonlight, his figure dark and forbidding. The muscles of his chest bunched as if he held himself back.

Why did he have to have a conscience now? It made her respect him and she didn't want that. She wanted to hate him for what he was making her do, make it his responsibility and not her own. But he wouldn't. And that meant she'd have to face the truth.

She might have feared this in the beginning, but no

longer. Now her disquiet came from knowing that she wanted him every bit as much as he wanted her.

She dragged her lip between her teeth as she realized she had not agreed to this because of Phoebe or her aunt or some slip of paper that threatened their existence. That had all been a convenient excuse.

She had come because of that first kiss. She had come to finish what they had started in that alley.

He raked his fingers through his thick hair. The bulging of the muscles of his arms made her stomach twitch. Her breath caught and her gaze flashed to his.

He moved closer. A band of moonlight illuminated his face, making his eyes glow unnaturally bright. He exuded an aura of primal power that struck her middle like a blow. But this was not fear, oh no, this was something far more powerful—far more dangerous. She wanted him to do those things to her—all of them.

He lifted a crooked finger and stroked her cheek. "Why can't I get past you?"

She placed a hand on his chest, feeling his warm, bare flesh and his heartbeat racing with her own. "The same reason I couldn't stay away. Damn you, Sam, for bringing me here."

"You want to go back?"

"I can't. I want you too much."

He lifted his face to the ceiling. "Thank God."

Chapter Twelve

An instant later he captured her, burying his strong fingers deep in her hair. Kate no longer fought his control but submitted to him completely.

Sam stared at her mouth.

She half closed her eyes and smiled up at him in open invitation. "Take me to bed, Sam."

He moved like a desperate man, sweeping her into his arms and holding her high against his chest. Then he charged out the back door as if retreating from gunfire. She felt the rush of cold air and then they were safe inside the sleeping coach.

Only when they reached the bed did he lower her feet to the carpet, but he kept one arm about her, trapping her beside him. This time she did not want to run.

The room was dark, private. She leaned against him and he pressed her close. He gripped her shoulders and she lifted her chin to look up at him, now the shadows making him appear almost sinister.

"What changed your mind?" he asked, giving her one last chance to escape. His hands still imprisoned her, as if he waged some colossal battle between his heart and head. Hadn't she done much the same? Only now she was through listening to the nagging whine of reason and heard only the call of her heart.

"You did, by giving me a taste of what we could share and then walking away," she whispered.

His touch branded her. Anticipation coiled tight within her belly as she lifted her mouth in a silent entreaty.

She threw herself into the kiss, the urgent embrace, the possessive slide of his hot tongue against the darting thrust of her own and the hard ridge of male flesh pressing against her yielding body. Her arms stole around his ribs and she nestled herself close, needing to feel the firm planes of his chest against the soft ache of her breasts.

A rumbling growl sounded in his throat, like the low, satisfied purr of a great mountain lion. He drew back, causing her to cry out at the loss of the warm and wonderful pressure. With quick expertise, he released the ribbon closure of her robe and slipped it from her shoulders.

She was surprised at her own impatience for the velvety glide of skin on skin.

He stepped away to drop his shirt on the floor beside her discarded robe. He tugged off his boots and trousers. He stood with his back to her for just a moment and she realized that he did not wear any underclothes at all. It confirmed her early assessment that this man had only the thinnest veneer of civility. Beneath the fine clothes, he was rough-edged, tough, and now she wanted to explore every one of those hard edges.

Her mouth went dry and her fingers itched to stroke the cording muscles of his wide back. He turned to face her, letting her see all.

She drew in a breath at the shock of being confronted by his erect male flesh. Her knees wobbled and she lowered herself to sit on the bed. This left her with an even closer view.

He dropped to a crouch before her. "Kate?"

Tentatively, she stroked the nest of dark, curling hair that covered his chest and then moved her hand to caress the warm velvet of his shoulder. The concern left his face, replaced by the fixed stare of a predator about to spring. He would no longer release her. She knew it in her soul. It had gone too far.

Thank God, she thought. Her entire body pulsed with a new and growing desire for him. She needed his hands on her as desperately as she needed the air in her lungs.

Warm fingers pushed her hem above her knee, his thumb drawing circles on the flesh of her inner thigh as he pulled the gauzy lace upward.

She gasped at the sensual pleasure and threw back her head to relish the hungry pressure as his mouth replaced his hand. Warm kisses and hungry strokes of his tongue moved up her thigh, causing the decadent tingling of arousal. She reached back to clasp the bedding, curling her fingers into claws as she wadded the velvet bedcover in her fist.

She felt the slick moisture between her legs and marveled at her need. It was like a madness.

"So soft," he whispered. "Oh, Kate, I've dreamed of this since the first moment I saw you."

She lowered her head found his dark eyes reflecting raw possessiveness. And still he kissed her, his gaze never leaving hers. Desire roared within her at the erotic sight of him nuzzling her inner thigh, his teeth scoring her tender flesh.

She found the contrast of her pale leg against his brawny arms excited her. She groaned and let herself fall backward onto the mattress. Tiny kisses pressed to her upper thigh as he crawled inch by delicious inch up her body.

Sam was on fire and alive for the first time in years. He experienced everything—the quivering of her flesh as his lips brushed along her leg, the soft downy hair sprinkling her thigh, the sweet taste of her skin and the arousing scent of her sex.

He stroked her and kissed her as he moved with slow deliberation. She arched to meet him as if longing for his touch.

He kissed the bony ridge of her pelvis through the thin lace of her nightgown, up the soft, gentle mound of her belly to the sharp angle of her ribs.

Her body was firm in the right places and soft and yielding in others. He pressed her down to the mattress with his hips as he continued to scale her body.

He throbbed with need for her, but longed to watch her face when she came. He stroked the soft swell of her breasts, spreading his fingers wide to claim her. Her breathing grew frantic. He wished he could see her more clearly as she arched and panted. Another time, he promised himself, for there would be a next time, and a next, he knew for certain. This was not a woman he could easily set aside. Oh, no. This was a woman to savor, cherish and keep. He untied the silver ribbons, opening the lace to reveal her white skin. He stroked her breasts and she arched to meet him, her nipples pebbling under his palms. He took one dark tip into his mouth, drawing and sucking. He reveled at her reaction, as she writhed beneath him like a madwoman. He had brought on the madness that was both torment and delight and all because he had waited for her to come to him.

And she had. Thank the Lord.

His hips pinned her and she arched her soft belly against his erection, making him gasp. How he wanted to drive into her now, again and again. He knew she was wet, ready.

Not yet. He'd see to her pleasure first.

He turned and captured her other nipple in his mouth, licking and sucking with rough strokes.

Mewling sounds came from deep in her throat and her fingers raked his back, clenching and unclenching in a rhythmic dance of need. He stroked her thigh, moving up to the short, curling hairs, finding her cleft silken and damp. Still he would not have her yet. He would watch her take her pleasure and in doing so he would increase his own. He meant to replace every bad memory she ever had with this fire that roared between them.

Her face glistened with moisture, making her skin shine like the surface of the moon.

She was impatient, tugging at his shoulders, scoring his back with her nails and lifting her hips insistently. It was a command he could not resist. He pressed her back to the mattress using his fingers to stroke her most sensitive places.

He knew she was close from the change in her breathing and the restless toss of her head. His fingers danced over her slick flesh as he watched her.

"Please, please," she cried.

He rolled away, reaching for the drawer beside his bed.

"What are you doing?" she asked, her voice breathless.

If he told her, it might cool her ardor. He reached for one of the paper packets and tore it open with his teeth, quickly sliding the thin skin sheath over his erection. Unlike his father—the bastard—he'd not bring another unwanted child into this world.

It took only a moment before he was beside her again, pressing her down to the bed, kissing her neck. She welcomed him, spreading her legs as he slipped between her thighs.

He poised himself at her cleft, restraining the need to thrust deep, as he eased slowly forward. Was her cry that of pleasure or pain? He closed his eyes and prayed he had not hurt her as he held himself motionless, waiting.

She wrapped her legs about his hips and drew them together in one sharp pull, removing all doubt. Something broke loose inside him. All his good intentions of gentle loving shattered inside him like glass. He gripped her buttocks, so she could not escape him, thrusting deeply into her soft, yielding body. Her passage was so tight and slick. He drove her down to the mattress again and again as he buried his face in the warm, sweet scent of her neck.

No, no, he had not wanted this. This was not the patient lover he had vowed to be.

"Faster," she cried.

He squeezed his eyes shut in relief and did as she commanded. For the first time he was glad for the thin skin sheath as it made it possible for him to last longer. Her gasps grew sharp and her strong legs scaled higher until she clung to his waist. She drove him mad. He moved faster as she met his driving force with yielding heat. Then she began an upward thrust of her own, gripping him with her legs, doubling the speed of the gliding friction between them.

He lifted to his elbows and captured her tossing head in his palms.

"Kate. Look at me. I want to see you come."

Her eyes flew open and he drove deep into her.

She stared up at him as he continued to plunge into her. Kate's eyes grew wide and her mouth dropped open as the cry erupted from her beautiful lips. He felt her rolling contraction, squeezing him. It was his undoing. He threw his head back and gritted his teeth against the rush of pleasure that poured through him as he came.

Her body went slack a moment before he collapsed upon her. She was so small he felt he might crush her. He used the last of his strength to roll aside, drag off the preventative before gathering her to his chest. She flopped against him like a child's rag doll.

Light from the moon cut a silver swath across the bed, making her damp skin glitter like diamonds and painting her dark hair silver. Her lips were swollen from his kisses. He traced the slight blue veins that feathered across her closed eyelids. She was more beautiful than ever at this moment.

Her eyelids fluttered and opened. Their eyes met. He held his breath. Never in his life had he wanted to have pleased a woman more. She gave him a smile of pure contentment. He felt her stretch, her toes curling against his legs. Her eyes dropped closed and she nestled to his chest. He grabbed the edge of the coverlet and flipped it over her, cradling her tight to his body.

She had initially intrigued him and his curiosity had led him to her door. His curiosity was now sated, but not his desire. Lord help him, it had grown even more keen. He feared he'd never get enough of her. How could a man ever grow tired of this?

His stomach knotted as he recognized that she was not a woman he could work out of his system, not a woman he would tire of, not a woman he could discard. Reflexively, his grip upon her tightened as he recognized that this was a woman he would defend against all challengers and keep as long as she would have him.

Infatuation. Perhaps that was what it had been. But it felt different than any other woman of his past. Just the thought of separating from Kate made him ache.

She had made it clear she did not want him permanently, making him delineate their severance agreement before he had even bedded her.

Her words echoed in his mind. *I have something more valuable than money. My independence.*

How did he convince her to stay? Marriage was the obvious way to claim a woman. He'd never thought to find one he wished to wed and now she'd robbed him of the possibility before he even considered it. She had so much as told him she would never marry again.

Sam stroked her hair from her face and kissed her brow as she slept. He wouldn't give her up, marriage or no. He didn't need her for a wife, so long as he could be with her.

You don't deserve her. You ain't fit for anyone, let alone a woman a fine as this.

His jaw clenched. He had told her about Randy and she had not been shocked. Kate had simply listened and sympathized without judging.

Don't be stupid. No woman would want a man who had done what you have.

Sam studied her sleeping form.

This woman might. This woman who knew the pain of loss, who had lived with the guilt of her sister's death and the brutality of marriage to Lawrence Wells. This woman had been forged in fire. A survivor—like him. She just might accept him, despite what he had done on this very mountain.

He closed his eyes and prayed he was right.

Chapter Thirteen

Kate basked in the glow of perfect satisfaction. Beneath her ear, Sam's heart beat a calm, steady rhythm. A wonderful lethargy made her feel heavy, as if filled with warm, wet sand. She had just enough energy to curl her lips into a smile.

How was it that a married woman was only now discovering the joys of the flesh? Her smile flickered as she recognized how jaded her opinions of men had become and how wrong.

She used one finger to stroke the nest of curling hair that ran down the center of Sam's chest. This man had given her a precious gift. He had seen to her pleasure and taught her things about her own body she never even suspected. She was worldly enough to know that this was rare. It made her wistful for things she would never have, like a life with Sam.

It was public knowledge that Sam Pickett never stayed with any woman for long. His trail of discarded liaisons was as legendary as was his firm affirmation to remain unattached. She did not doubt that their affair would end, now that the chase had ended. How long until his ardor cooled?

She had offered a challenge, perhaps, but his conquest of her had been complete. They would share a few days or weeks and then he would send her off with a parting gift to soften the blow. Mistresses had no protection, but neither did they have any obligation to stay with a man who mistreated them. Wasn't that what she wanted?

Twenty-four hours ago she had believed with her whole heart that her autonomy was her greatest possession, but at this moment she felt uncertain. Freedom was a gift, but it seemed cold company compared to the comfort she found in this man's arms.

Kate clung to him, fighting the drowsiness that crept over her until she yielded, at last, to sleep.

She woke in the morning to discover they had not drawn the blinds. Sunlight streamed in, filling the chamber with rosy light.

She shifted, rolling away from Sam. But he followed, turning to his side and gathering her so that his chest blanketed her back. He curled his legs and her bottom pressed into his lap. Then he began to stroke her.

She found her voice was low and hoarse. "Well, no wonder."

"No wonder, what?" His voice had the appealing grumble of a sleepy man.

"No wonder you can have any woman you like."

He chuckled. "You thought it was the money?"

"Of course."

He cupped her breast. "I'm not the only man who can do that, you know."

She slid her foot along his shin. "Perhaps not, but you're the only one who has ever done it to me."

"Want me to do it again?"

She nodded. "Definitely."

He drew the lacy gown from her shoulders. She turned to assist him. Then he tossed it aside casually.

"Do you know how much that cost?" she asked, failing to sound as stern as she intended.

"Worth every penny. Only thing I'd rather see you in is nothing at all."

He flipped back the coverlet to see her in the morning light. She had never been shy or prim, just cautious of men and their appetites. But Sam had changed all that. She watched his eyes devour her and the muscles of his jaw clench. He wanted her again and that suited her.

She gave a long, languid stretch and a low rumble emanated from his throat.

He stroked down the center of her breastbone from her throat to her navel.

"So beautiful," he whispered.

He lay on his side caressing her with feathery touches, while she admired the thick muscles of his torso and the dark curling hair that covered his chest. His leg was thrown possessively across her hips so she could not see all of him, but she could feel him, growing hard, pressing against her thigh.

Soon the touches were not enough. She writhed against him and he smiled in satisfaction. His mouth moved to her neck and then down to her breasts. She grew more anxious for him until her impatience caused her to grasp at his hip and pull.

He laughed and she struck him on the shoulder with her open hand.

"Brute."

"Impatient wench," he countered.

Then he rolled to his back and folded his hands behind his head. "You want it? Take it."

What did that mean? Did he expect her to drag him over her like a coverlet? She was flummoxed.

His forehead wrinkled. "Kate, you know that you can take me, as well, don't you?"

Now she felt stupid, ignorant as a virgin. Her cheeks grew hot.

"Here now," he said, stroking her face. "I'll show you."

He slid to the edge of the bed for a moment, opened a drawer and returned with a paper packet, which he handed to her. Then he lay beside her on his back.

"What is this?" she asked.

"It's a skin sheath. It covers me so you won't have a baby."

She dropped the thing as if it were on fire.

"That's immoral." She then recalled that sleeping with a man outside of marriage was equally immoral.

His brow descended. "No. Immoral is bringing an unwanted child into the world."

Unwanted—like he was. She understood it all now. He was trying to protect her. Trying to keep another child from suffering what he had suffered.

"Yes, that's so."

"Do you want me to use it or would you rather risk the alternative?"

She took up the packet again. "Use it."

He tore it open and showed her how to put it on him. It looked uncomfortable.

He clasped her hips and pulled her up until she straddled his thighs. She lay across his chest, her belly pressing his erection flat between them.

"Sit up," he urged.

She did. He placed his hands at her waist urging her up. She rose to her knees and suddenly it all became clear.

"Oh!" she said.

"Oh," he repeated, and gave her a devilish smile.

She lowered herself onto him. The sensation of settling over him was so pleasurable she gasped. She sank lower, relishing the sliding friction as he filled her. She noted that the smile had left his face and his muscles were now knotted in an effort to keep still.

She liked the control this position afforded her and the power to make him wait. She smiled down at him.

"Now what?" she asked, and then spoiled it by laughing.

His mouth quirked, but he did not manage a smile. "Now you start to move or I throw you onto your back."

"Ah, an ultimatum. I choose the former." She lifted her hips and began a slow rocking. Sam's eyes closed and he arched to the mattress.

The muscles of his throat corded and he ground his teeth. It appeared as if she was torturing him. She leaned forward until her swaying breasts swept over his chest. He groaned.

She bared her teeth and scored his neck, then moved to do to him what he had done to her. She licked his flat nipple and was astonished to see it bud, just as hers had done. She sucked it and the growl grew louder.

His hands came up to capture her hips. She straightened, realizing he was no longer in a mood to play. He began to move, lifting up as he held her down. Again and again he bucked against her. She arched back, trusting him to hold her, as the cresting wave built within her once more. She cried out as she came and his cry followed just behind her own. He held her still as he locked himself deep inside her.

She fell forward onto his chest, gasping. He stroked the tangle of her hair.

"Glorious. I've never seen anything more beautiful than that," he murmured in her ear.

She slid from him and nestled close to his side, dozing for a time. She woke when she felt the bed sag. Kate pushed the hair from her face and blinked.

Sam sat beside her on the bed, already shaved and dressed. He stood to strap on his black holster and pistol, then noticed her and smiled.

He leaned down to kiss her. "I'm off to get us some breakfast. Get dressed and meet me in the next coach." He secured his hat and then seemed to remember something. "We're going up the line to our sawmill today. We have to leave the compartment to reach it, so wear something you can ride in."

With that he was off. Kate felt a creeping resentment. She'd just spent the most fabulous night of her life with Sam, but in the morning light he was already dictating what she should wear, when she would eat and where she would go. She was to be the ornament on his arm again today. It was a role she thought to play so easily, but her hatred of the task meddled with her intentions.

What did she expect? She had sold her independence for a necklace of gold. This man, like all men, was used to treating women like cattle, something to be tended and prodded and used.

But this time, she had not given over the bill of sale. The arrangement was temporary. As soon as she had word that her aunt had paid their debts, she would tell Mr. Pickett he could find someone else to dress up like a porcelain doll.

Kate again faced the challenge of dressing alone. The man seemed to have no notion of the complications such an arrangement entailed. Their agreement had specifically included servants, but thus far none had been provided. She was desperate for a lady's maid and planned to speak to him about it.

In the meantime she laced the back of her corset and then used the front laces to cinch herself in.

The crisp white blouse and petticoats were simple to don, as was the riding habit. It was no more complicated than a jacket and skirts, except the skirts cut just to the ankle. As she stood before the glass, she studied the rich golden velvet of the habit and realized with chagrin that she looked as if she had dressed to match the bed curtains.

The train shuddered. Then the whistle shrieked and smoke billowed past the windows. A moment later the cars began to roll.

When she had regained her equilibrium, she lifted the hat that included a black lace train and veil, should she encounter insects. She secured the hat with her new pins and then gave herself one final inspection. She looked well kept.

She glared at her reflection and stormed toward the passage between the cars.

She found Sam waiting in the adjoining coach with his breakfast half-finished. It was very impolite to eat without her, but she remembered where he had been raised and held her tongue.

He did stand when he saw her and smiled broadly. "That color makes your hair look even redder."

"It's auburn, silly."

He motioned to the place where she should sit and poured her coffee. She preferred tea. She had not noticed the servant beside the bar until he presented a gargantuan breakfast and then withdrew. The meal was better suited to a laborer than a lady wearing an overly tight corset. She ignored the bloody steak, beans and fried eggs, longing for a bit of toast and jam.

"I've got some appetite this morning," said Sam as he finished everything on his plate and then downed his coffee in three long swallows. He glanced at her untouched meal. "What's wrong?"

"I usually have a pot of tea in the morning. I'll never fit into my new clothes if I eat that."

"Oh, hmm. Tea, huh? Just tea?"

"With milk and sugar."

"Hmm." He was thoughtful a moment. "Well, I'll see about tea with lunch. How's that?"

"Lovely."

"I've sent word ahead. Told them to pick you out a nice gentle mare."

"That's very thoughtful of you. But despite my appearances, I cannot ride."

"You…what?"

"I've never ridden a horse. But perhaps you thought that buying me a riding habit and then securing a mare would make an equestrian of me."

He sat back in utter astonishment. Then a line formed between his eyebrows as he stared at her. Kate regretted her words as memories of Luke's temper flashed in her mind like lightning. Sam reached for her and she pulled it back as fast as she could, bracing against the seat back.

"I'm not gonna hurt you, Kate."

She found she could breathe again. When she glanced up it was to find him staring, his expression more concern than fury. She lowered her head, ashamed at her ingratitude. She stared at the cup of coffee. "I apologize for being churlish."

"This is about the tea, ain't it?"

She shook her head. "I don't think so."

"Then you lost me a ways back."

Her sigh was cut short by the corset stays. "Sam, I have worked every day for nearly a year. And while it is true I cannot do just as I like much of the time, I do have a certain autonomy. I choose what I eat, for instance, and what I wear. In the summer I have toast, and in the winter I eat oatmeal in the mornings."

Sam made a face. "I ain't touched the stuff since I ran away."

Of course an orphanage would serve such fare. She imagined it was not the lovely concoction she made.

"I make mine with brown sugar, nuts and raisins. It's delicious."

"Accept your word on that." He rubbed his jaw. "You having trouble taking the bit, then. That it?" He rubbed his chin as he stared at her. "I recall a time when I got told when to sleep, eat, work. Never liked it, either." He smiled.

"You're not angry?"

"Put out, you might say. I never had a full-time woman. Kinda figured they were too much trouble." He gave her a meaningful look and she felt her face heat. "You want your own say-so. But you're mine for now and I have to see to your needs as best I can. That means sometimes you do what I tell you."

She didn't like it, but she nodded. "I understand."

"So I'm telling you to eat something, 'cause it will be hours before we see anything else."

She stared at her plate and decided the eggs were the least offensive. She ate half of the portion and then choked down some of the coffee.

"Was that so bad?" he asked.

She winced at the bitter taste in her mouth and he chuckled.

"I'll get a wagon for you and a driver for today. Can't guarantee a carriage once we reach the work camps. It's pretty rough there. But we got lots of Chinese workers so I guess there'll be plenty of tea." He reached for her hand again and she did not try to deny him.

"I got a gift for you."

Kate wondered if she could sell it, as well, and sat

forward on her seat. "Really. I don't deserve one after this morning."

His gaze turned heated and her heart rate sped up. "But you do after last night."

She blushed, but said nothing as he reached for the overcoat on the empty chair beside him. In a moment he drew out a large envelope.

Not jewelry, she realized with dismay, but then was thankful. If he had given her earrings to match the necklace he would be disconcerted not to see the set.

He handed it over and sat back to watch her open the gift. Inside she found a beautifully etched certificate for one hundred shares of the Union Pacific Railroad.

"You're a shareholder now, Kate. You keep that a while. It's bound to be worth a fortune someday."

She had no idea what else she could do with it, so she'd likely follow his advice. She had already been extremely rude this morning, so she covered her disappointment, pressing the certificate to her heart as if it was something precious, instead of a finely decorated bit of paper.

"Oh, thank you, Sam! You are a generous man." She stood to kiss him and he drew her onto his lap.

"Hey," he said. "Where's the necklace?"

She bit her lip. Here was her second opportunity to admit she had left it behind with her aunt. Instead, she smiled at him.

"With a riding habit? Honestly, Sam, you know nothing about women's fashions."

She waited to see if he would let the matter pass. Luke most certainly would not have. He would have insisted she wear it and there would be hell to pay if she did not produce it.

Sam smiled at her. "Ain't that the truth."

Allen Crawford of the Pinkerton Detective Agency arrived in Cole's office unexpectedly, but Cole showed him in immediately.

"Police found the other woman from the alley. She pulled the same stunt on a fellow down by the river and they grabbed her. I'm going to question her about Katherine Wells."

Cole frowned. "You suspect something."

"That's what you pay me for. I'm not much for coincidences. Mrs. Wells has earned herself a lucrative spot beside a powerful man, due in large part to her *timely* arrival. It smells of a setup, not to rob Pickett, but to present Mrs. Wells to him in a nearly irresistible manner."

"I'll be damned."

Chapter Fourteen

Sam managed to find a small wagon with a mule and an Irishman to drive Kate to the building site. Sam sent his cartographers and surveyors ahead, escorted by three Pinkertons, with instructions to verify the potential new route. Although Sam had wanted to run the railroad straight through Broadner Pass, he was a realist. That meant taking the course with the most favorable grade.

Sam glanced back at Kate to find her sitting primly beside her driver. He was sorry he had spoiled their morning by simply ordering up two breakfasts. How did he know what a woman ate in the morning?

Sam wrestled with the balance between care and control. He'd never met a woman so touchy on the subject. The ladies he had known loved to be pampered and spoiled. Kate seemed to be cut from a different cloth. He liked it, but it confused him.

They reached the lower camp below the sawmill by

midday. The afternoon was unseasonably warm and Kate looked flushed and about done in in her heavy velvets. He needed to push on and get to the mill to see about beefing up the security. He was about to tell her she'd wait here for his return when he hesitated.

"It's another hour up to the mill by wagon. You want to come along or wait for me here?"

Kate paused a moment as she realized he was leaving the choice up to her. Beneath her jacket and shirt, a bead of sweat rolled down her back. She glanced about. This was a lovely place, with the river tamed by the dam so only a gentle stream danced past. The tall pines on the wide banks gave pleasant shade and the millpond above them made this former riverbed a new meadow already cloaked in wildflowers.

"When will you be back?" she asked.

"Before supper."

She glanced up the steep grade that held two switch-backs and then stared up at him. "I'll wait, if it's all right with you."

He dismounted and assisted her down. "I'll see you set up and then head off."

"You go on. I can see to myself."

He looked skeptical and then bit back his words. If she said she could do it, he'd let her go.

"Tell the men to set us up a tent and order something for dinner. I'll be back before full dark."

He kissed her and then remounted. Then he headed over to speak to John Potts, a foreman at the camps, who Sam had recruited from his mine. He trusted him and that was why he ordered him to stay back with Kate.

She might like the illusion of autonomy, but when it came to brass tacks, a woman needed a protector, especially out here.

"Help her get organized, will you, John? And keep an eye on her." Sam glanced at the man's revolver.

Potts gave a nod of understanding, then he looked back at Kate. "I'll take good care of her."

"And get her a pot of tea."

"Tea?"

"With milk and sugar."

John scratched his head. "Sugar's no problem, but where am I gonna get milk up here?"

"Just find some."

"Okay, Chief."

Sam waved at Kate and pressed his heels into his horse's sides.

Kate watched him disappear after the others. He'd left her in charge of making camp. She smiled in satisfaction and then set to work organizing the gear they had carried from the train. In short order his assistant had erected the tent on a sturdy wood floor. The canvas sides were low, but the center was high enough to stand up in and the overlarge flooring made a porch of sorts. Here she stood as the carpet, chairs, table and cots were brought in and arranged to her orders. She didn't fancy sleeping on a cot, but perhaps she could sleep on Sam again.

That thought made her smile. It felt wonderful to have something to do. About midafternoon, John Potts arrived with a steaming coffeepot.

"Oh, thank you, John, but I don't drink coffee."

"It's gunpowder tea, according to the Chinaman I bought it off of."

Kate clapped her hands in delight. An instant later she realized who must have arranged this.

"Mr. Pickett asked you for this. Didn't he?"

"Yes, ma'am. Thought the milk would skin me, but I found some." He was positively glowing with pride.

"You are an angel. Thank you, John."

Kate sat at the table before the dented coffeepot whose base was black with soot. She glanced about.

"Where is the milk?" she asked John.

"I already added a can full of condensed milk to the pot."

Kate's hopes fell.

"Here's the sugar." Potts handed over a paper packet, neatly folded and tied with string, setting it beside the odd ceramic cup that stood only two inches high and had no handle.

Kate forced a smile.

"What a strange cup."

"Got that from a Chinaman, too. He said that I shouldn't put no milk in this tea, but Mr. Pickett said to find you milk, so I did."

And had likely ruined the tea. Kate didn't have the heart to tell him that as she poured herself a cup. The concoction was pale and vicious. Dark tea leaves appeared and disappeared like tiny frogs surfacing for air.

Potts leaned in. "Is that how it's supposed to look?"

"Not precisely." Kate removed her white gloves, setting them carefully upon the table. Then she lifted the squat ceramic cup and resisted the urge to hold her nose. She took a sip. Dreadful.

"Perfect," she said, and beamed at him.

John turned scarlet and for a moment she thought he was choking, but he recovered himself.

"But perhaps, next time, I could add the milk to each cup."

Potts' eyes rounded as he considered this. She was quite certain he understood that he had done something wrong now. Some of his pride leaked away and he stood blinking at her like a large grizzly bear that she had slapped on the nose. She felt quite sorry for him and sorry for the lovely tea, ruined by canned milk.

He stammered. "Is there anything else I can get you?"

"No, thank you. And John, I certainly appreciate the tea."

He grinned, showing a broken front tooth, and then backed away as if she was royalty.

Kate lifted the tea, holding it before her lips until he turned his back, and then she threw it off the porch.

She sat back in the folding chair, thinking her bottom would never recover from the jostling she had taken on the wagon ride. But here in the shade, she had a lovely view of the bubbling stream. Funny that there would be such huge boulders in such a small body of water. She glanced upstream but could see nothing of the dam or lumber mill.

All about her the green grass shared the meadow with pink and white lupine. The scene was so pictureSque she wished she had her paint box, not that she could do it justice. She smiled, feeling relaxed for the first time today. Pity about the tea, though.

A booming sound rumbled down the mountain, sending vibrations through her feet. She stood, wondering if a thundercloud had crept in behind her, but saw nothing but blue sky. Storms were sudden and violent in the mountains and she had no desire to soak her new riding outfit. Could it be behind the ridge?

If it were not a storm, what could have caused such a sound?

John appeared, craning his neck this way and that as he tried to locate the source. His unease was contagious. Kate reached for her reticule, slipping it over her wrist. She always felt better with her derringer at hand.

A moment later she thought she heard a low rumble, like an approaching train, but it did not abate. Instead, it grew louder and louder.

She glanced at Mr. Potts and found him looking upstream, his eye round with shock. Her heart jumped in her chest as she realized what the sound could mean.

Sam caught the Pinkertons as they headed up the final quarter mile of the lumber road. They were just discussing vulnerable points to the mill when the explosion shook them.

There was no mistaking the source as a blast of dynamite. Sam turned toward the dam and watched in horror as it fell away before the eruption of water.

"Kate!"

He wheeled his horse about.

"Mr. Pickett, you can't go that way. We have to stay on the high ground."

But he was already spurring his gelding and leaning

low over his neck. He called back to them. "Go catch the bastards!"

The men took off at a gallop in the opposite direction. The cascade of water and debris roared down the narrow canyon, filling it with terrifying speed and then sloshing up and over the road like water over the lip of a washtub.

The horse was solid, continuing on at a gallop even when the water reached his hocks. Despite Sam's speed, he could not match the river. It ricocheted down the canyon, ripping trees from the banks and dragging them into the rolling torrent of destruction.

And all of it was heading right at Kate.

It was John Potts who recognized first the meaning behind the sound. He grabbed Kate's hand and dragged her off the raised platform. Somehow she kept her footing as they ran perpendicular to the stream.

Potts shouted to the cook and the others as they ran. "The dam's gone! Run for it, boys!"

At his words, Kate felt a sharp stab of fear.

"Sam," she called, trying to turn in the direction he had gone. But Mr. Potts had a firm hold and did not let her go.

"Hurry, ma'am."

She slowed and he tugged, turning to her in frustration. She pointed, calling over the increasing roar. "Sam's up there!"

"Above the dam. Safe!" he shouted. "Now run or the water will kill us both!"

She ran for her life as her mind filled with the terrors of drowning. She could not swim and even if she could, she knew that the heavy, sodden velvet would drag her down.

She grew dizzy from the effort to breathe against the constraints of her corset. But when she slowed, Potts tugged and shouted. She glanced back to see only the quiet stream, but just north of the bend the trees were falling.

My God, they'd never survive.

Potts released her to scramble up the rocky embankment, and she feared he had abandoned her. But then he turned and hauled her up. Men charged past them on both sides, but Potts stayed behind, faithful as a hound. She didn't deserve such loyalty and could only imagine that it was Sam who had earned this man's devotion.

She wanted to tell him to go on without her, but she was a coward. She wanted to live.

Who would take care of Phoebe if she died? Where was Sam? The water careened across the meadow reaching for them as they sought higher ground.

Potts was behind her now, pushing and shouting. The others were gone. She scraped her palms on the rocks as she grabbled up the steep slope.

"The trees! Climb, Mrs. Wells!"

She had her arms around the trunk of a huge pine. The sturdy branches hung overhead, impossibly high.

Potts was beside her now. "Come on, missus!"

He braced his back against the tree and offered his clasped hands as if she were mounting a mare instead of a pine tree. She placed her boot in his cupped hands and rose as if by magic. The lower branches were suddenly within reach. She wrapped her fingers around the limbs and pulled. The buttons of her fine short coat tore. Below her, Potts pushed at her foot and she managed to get her torso over the branch.

Muddy water washed around the base of the pine like a wave. Potts lost his footing and fell.

"John!"

He was up again, clawing at the rocks as the water chased him. He scrambled to his feet as Kate watched in horror. If not for her, he'd be safely up the bank with the others. It was her fault he was overcome.

Potts was dragged down by the swelling torrent and then thrown against the trunk of a tree. He disappeared below the dirty water and Kate screamed.

She scanned the rising flood but could not find him. Then she spied a flash of blue flannel. He hugged a tree trunk as the water rushed past him. She called to him as he tried and failed to scramble up the evergreen. The water continued to surge. In a moment it would be over his head, but still he held on, tenacious as a tick on a dog.

Kate looked below her with alarm. The water was now only a few feet beneath her dangling legs. When she looked back at John, she saw him release his hold, thrashing his arms and kicking madly along with the current. In an instant, he had vanished from her sight. Her heart twisted in horror.

"No!"

But he was gone. Water splashed onto her boots. She bent her legs and wiggled forward until she managed to throw one leg over the branch. It was then that she noticed the end of her branch was now dragging in the water. The pine needles trailed into the flood and the branch was bent at a dangerous angle. Kate scrambled to stand on her narrow perch, but her skirt snagged. Water splashed over her legs, soaking the velvet.

Panic froze her to the spot as she imagined herself sucked under the muddy water.

"No!"

She tore at the hooks closing her skirts to her waist, peeling out of her velvet and then tugging at the series of petticoats. One, two, three. The strings tangled. Her fingernails bent and tore. She released a cord. The first garments fell away and then the next until she stood in nothing but her bloomers and her tattered coat. Her reticule had moved up her arm and now hung around her shoulder like the braided aiguillette on a military uniform. She left it there as it did not hinder her movements.

Now she was light and agile. She climbed up and up, praying that the roots would hold and for protection from the muddy death that swirled beneath her feet.

The branch on which she had first stood disappeared and then the next followed. She hugged the trunk, pressing her forehead against the rough bark as she clung. Her hands were sticky with tree sap and blood. She closed her eyes and prayed that Sam had escaped, that John would survive and finally that her pine would hold.

Chapter Fifteen

The flood forced Sam to higher ground. It slowed him as he navigated the hillside above what had once been the road. That was how he happened upon his men standing just above the high-water mark. He felt a moment's rush of joy until he scanned them for a patch of gold velvet. Kate was not among them.

Sam pulled up on the reins, skidding to a halt before Everett MacPherson, a longtime employee, first at the mine and then with the railroad.

"Where is she?"

Everett stared hopelessly at the swirling water. "She and Potts were right behind us."

"You left her?" Rage welled inside him and he fought the murderous urge to kick Everett into the torrent.

No one spoke. Sam stared out at the destruction before him and then back to his men.

"Search downstream. Don't come back until you find them or hit Sacramento."

The man scrambled down the rocks to the shore. The rage and impotence congealed in Sam's throat. Why had he left her? She was his responsibility and he had failed to protect her. He drew a ragged breath and shouted her name again and again.

He was torn between following the men in their search downstream and staying here where he had seen her last. The waters were receding, creeping back down the slope leaving mud, branches and broken timber behind.

His heart sank, twisting and burning his chest. He gritted his teeth against the fury that threatened to carry him away like the floodwater.

First his mother, then his brother and now Kate.

He thought she might stay, might understand. But God had taken her, too. The black storm was back and churning within him like a cyclone. He didn't care about anything or anyone. He was the wounded animal who wanted only to fight his enemy to the death. But this adversary was not one he could battle.

She was gone. He'd be lucky to be able to bring her body home to her family. Oh, Lord, her poor sister. Sam knew what she would suffer, for he knew the sorrow of the one left behind.

The dirty river gradually lost its power. Still, he could not seem to leave this place, refusing to accept that she was gone. He watched the grasses and branches float by, their speed now diminished to a normal current. He nudged his mount forward, following the retreating water.

Sam scanned the pines, submerged up to their lower branches and wondered if someone could have survived there.

The branches of sugar pines and ponderosa were too high for anyone to reach. But closer to the bank he recognized the rounded tops of several digger pines. These were easier to scale, with low, sturdy branches. Easy, that was, if you weren't wearing heavy velvet and God only knows how many petticoats.

Though he feared it was futile, he continued to call to her.

He paused to listen. At first he thought the sound was the high keen of a hawk, but he followed it moving upstream along the emerging bank. When he realized the call came from the cluster of digger pines he felt a moment's hope.

He held his breath and listened, but the cry had stopped. Then he noted a flash of white among the green and brown branches. It was the size of a swan.

"Kate!"

The thing moved and he saw a narrow band of golden velvet streaked with mud. What he'd mistaken for the tree trunk was her torso. Kate stood on a branch two feet above the water.

"Sam!"

"Don't move. I'm coming for you."

Sam spurred his horse, taking him upstream, and then plunged into the freezing water. His sorrel thrashed his front legs, swimming with the current but tangling in the submerged branches. Sam recognized that he could not control the horse's course any more than the gelding could and so he dropped his stirrups and pushing off the saddle, diving headfirst into the current.

Sam swam toward Kate, ignoring the lower branches

that clawed at his legs. The current threw him into a tree, stunning him momentarily, but he managed to grasp one of the branches before the river dragged him off. It bent as the river took him downstream and he feared he might shoot right by her.

No, that would not happen. Not when he was so close. He held his breath and released his hold, pumping his arms and thrashing his legs against the current. Despite his efforts, he missed the trunk, but managed to clasp one of the submerged branches, halting his momentum with a jolt. He surfaced just below her and found Kate climbing down the branches to reach him.

"Stop!" he ordered. She did.

He submerged again and used the sturdy limb to haul himself, hand over hand toward the treetrunk. The current slowed on the downstream side of the trunk and he was able to stand on the branch.

Kate was now at eye level. It seemed she had halted her descent only until his head disappeared below the water. He felt a tug on the back of his jacket and realized she had a hold of him and was trying to heave him from the water with one hand.

He grinned at her. "You going to pull me up or am I going to pull you down?"

"Well, you're not going under the water again." She said it like a vow.

He could have kissed her.

Instead, he stared up at her, taking in her brown boots, torn stockings, the bloomers he'd mistaken for a swan and the coat that was missing every button. Her little bag was slung over her shoulder, the ribbons drawn tight. Her hands were scraped, but somehow she had maintained her hat and veil in perfect order.

"Nice hat," he said.

She scowled at him. "Are you coming up?"

"Reckon so."

He heaved himself to the next branch as she retreated to the adjacent one.

Sam reached for her hand, clasping it gently. She winced.

"Thank you for not dying," he said.

Tears filled her eyes. "You can thank John Potts. He pushed me up into this tree and then…" She wept.

"We'll find him," Sam said. But he thought they might more likely find his body. If the man was alive, Sam owed him a debt he could never repay.

"Sam, how will we get down?"

"Wait a while. The water's receding fast now."

"What happened?" she asked.

He told her that someone had blown the dam and how he suspected the same men who had been stealing their supplies and shooting any worker who wandered from camp.

"Who would do such a thing?"

"More than a few shippers in 'Frisco will be sunk when the railroad's complete."

"They'd commit murder to stay in business?"

"That's right."

Kate's brows sank over her penetrating green eyes. "I think that's despicable. I hope you catch them and bring them all to justice."

"That's what I'm aiming to do. Right after I get us down from this damn tree."

She gave the branch a little pat. "This tree saved my life."

"Maybe I'll cut it down and make you a rocker to remember it by."

"Don't you dare! This tree did not survive the flood only to be carved into furniture."

He laughed. "If you say so. What about a branch? I'll whittle you something."

She nodded her consent. The woman had strong notions about things that never occurred to him. He found her views refreshing and her spunk admirable. But sometimes he wished she would do what he told her.

"What happened to your skirts?"

"They were dragging me down so I threw them into the river."

"Should have known."

"Known what?"

"Most women would have just let go. But not you. You'd strip naked if you had to."

"I believe I already have."

"You still got most of the top half, and that hat."

"I love this hat."

He grinned. "Water's nearly at the base. We can climb down now."

He helped her as they descended.

Sam called up to Kate as she hung from a branch. "You know them bloomers have a slit in them at the crotch?"

Kate froze to the spot and clamped her legs together. Sam laughed.

"You are a dreadful man. And to think I prayed for your safety."

That struck him. "You did?"

She nodded.

"I don't think I've been mentioned to God in quite some time." While she had prayed, he had cursed His name. They may both be survivors, but they were not alike in *all* things. She was a better person and, just maybe, she could make him a better person, as well. He realized something in that moment, staring up at her in her tattered clothing and mud-streaked bloomers. *He loved her.*

This was the woman he'd been searching for: the one he didn't think existed, the one that he dreamed of and the one he had nearly lost today. Now he had to convince her that her independence was not as precious as what they might share together. He would give her the world, if she'd only let him.

She sat on the lower branch and reached out to him. He clasped her waist and drew her to stand beside him in the ankle-deep mud.

Should he tell her now or ease into it at a better moment?

"Sam?"

He lifted his eyebrows.

"Thank you for rescuing me." She glanced downstream. "Do you really think John is alive?"

John? A burn began in his gut and traveled to his jaw. He clenched his teeth against the resentment. The man had saved her life. He owed him everything and yet

when she said his name with such concern, Sam wanted
to punch John Potts square in the teeth.

"We'll find him," Sam promised.

The police had done a thorough job on this case.
They'd apprehended the third thief who had waylaid Mr.
Pickett and they had found, in her possession, a valuable
gold necklace.

Crawford had tracked track down the jeweler and discovered that Sam Pickett had purchased the piece only
a few days earlier. How had this thief come into possession of the necklace?

The detective now sat in a small room with the
apparent thief. He placed the velvet box before the
young woman who was charged with luring men into
an alley so her cohorts could rob them.

"Miss Burns, do you care to tell me how this came
into your possession?"

"Mr. Pickett give it to me as a token of his affections."

Crawford smiled. He had just completed an initial inter-
view of a woman named Mrs. Ella Maguire, the maternal
aunt of Miss Katherine Wells. She had reported a house
robbery where only one item was taken, a gold necklace,
set with seven gold filigree roses. She reported that a
young woman had inquired about renting a room and had
used the tour of the premises as an opportunity to secure
the necklace. Mrs. Maguire had told the officers that the
necklace belonged to her niece but could produce no proof.

Crawford turned to the officer. "Bring in Mrs.
Maguire."

The older woman was escorted in. She wore a rumpled

gray jacket that looked as if it had been hastily dragged out from under a bed, and brown skirts with a tattered hem. Her eyes were cloudy, but it seemed she recognized Miss Burns.

She pointed at his suspect. "That's her!"

"Mrs. Maguire, is this the necklace?" He opened the box to display the delicate trinket, fashioned from eighteen-carat gold.

The woman leaned forward, squinting her eyes. "Yes. That's it. Oh, thank the Lord."

She reached for the box and he closed it.

"I'm sorry, Mrs. Maguire. This is now evidence."

"But it belongs to my niece."

"So you say, but this woman insists that it belongs to her. I understand your niece works in a milliner's shop on 2nd Street. Could you tell me how she came to own such an expensive necklace?"

Mrs. Maguire flushed. "I'm not at liberty to say."

"I see. Is it possible that Mr. Pickett gave it to her?"

The woman kept her mouth shut.

"Well, this is a dilemma. Both your niece and Miss Burns were together in that alley with Mr. Pickett and each woman claims this—" he tapped the box with his index finger "—belongs to her. Is your niece acquainted with Miss Burns?"

"Of course not!"

"And do you know all of your niece's acquaintances?"

"Kate would have nothing to do with a woman of this sort."

"I hadn't realized that Mr. Pickett's mistress traveled only in the upper circles."

The older woman turned scarlet, but did not deny his charge.

"Why was did your niece enter that alley?"

"She was responding to a citizen in need."

Crawford shook his head. "An unlikely happenstance, don't you agree, for a lady to enter an alley *at night* under any circumstances. And quite a coincidence for Mrs. Wells to be so close at hand with her derringer exactly when Mr. Pickett was waylaid."

"What are you implying, sir?"

"I don't believe in chance, Mrs. Maguire. Kate Wells, and Miss Burns here, were working to swindle Mr. Pickett. They concocted this encounter to present Miss Wells to Mr. Pickett, offering exactly the kind of woman he finds most appealing. A woman beautiful, brave and selfless." He turned to Miss Burns who nodded her agreement to his theory. "But she didn't split her take with you, did she, Miss Burns? So you went back for your due."

"It was Kate's idea. The whole thing. All I did was ask him to step out with me. I had no idea until afterward that Kate had made arrangements with those ruffians. And then she fired her pistol. I could have been killed." She lifted her chin and struck a haughty pose. "I'm innocent."

Crawford snorted. Miss Burns sank back into her seat to pout.

"Mr. Crawford," said the older woman. "I must insist you return the necklace. It belongs to my niece and she has left it in my custody."

"No, Mrs. Maguire. Until I hear otherwise, this necklace belongs to Mr. Pickett."

Chapter Sixteen

After the river had sufficiently receded, Sam carried Kate to safety. But the water was hip deep in places, so they were thoroughly soaked when they reached dry ground. He had a devil of a time finding his horse. Just when he decided to give up his search downstream, his whistle was answered by a frantic series of whinnies. He found his sorrel by a debris pile, muddy and shivering, ears perked as he whinnied for help. He had almost reached the bank when his reins snagged, leaving him stranded in water up to his hocks.

Sam whistled again and the gelding pawed at the water and tossed his head.

It was hard to say which of them was most grateful to see the other. Sam had him free in a matter of minutes, and then he helped Kate up to the waterlogged saddle. The beast would be lucky not to have several saddle sores from the wet blanket and muddy girth, but there was no helping it until they reached the sawmill.

Sam mounted behind Kate and steered them back up

what was left of the raised gravel log road. Kate's teeth were clattering and he felt warm only where his chest pressed to her back. Once they were within sight of the camp, he called for a blanket for Kate. She was bundled off to the foreman's cabin and into the charge of Grace Mackenzie, the foreman's wife.

Next, he sent a heavily armed search party after John Potts.

Finally, Sam headed for what had been their millpond. It had actually been more of a deep, narrow lake in what had once been a gorge cut between two steep cliffs. Even he was surprised by the amount of water they had captured.

He made a quick inspection with the foreman, noting that the mill wheel was now high and dry but intact. The dam had been obliterated.

One of the Pinkertons returned at a gallop. "They left a man behind. He was injured in the explosion."

"How bad?"

"He's dying, sir."

"Take me to him."

"We won't make it in time."

"Did he say anything?"

"Yes, sir. He said they were hired by Robert Donahue."

"Donahue!" Sam might have known. The man was among his most vocal opponents, with a reputation for bending the law that stretched back to the gold rush when he'd manned his vessels by shanghaiing unsuspecting men from the docks.

"Do you want us to pursue the others, stay to guard the mill or split our forces and do both?"

"Send them to guard the work camps."

"I suggest a detail of at least two men for your personal safety, sir."

He was about to object and then he remembered Kate. "Fine. Post them outside the foreman's house."

"Yes, sir."

"And get me someone who can ride. I need to send a wire."

The man bobbed his head again and set off. Before he made his way back to the foreman's cabin, a rider approached, ready to carry Sam's message to Cole.

Sam paused at the door to the cabin. Yesterday, he had kept Kate in grand style and today he'd nearly killed her. His jaw clenched as he recognized that he didn't know the first thing about how to protect her. He was good with burrowing in the earth and at making money. But this…

Would she forgive him for what he had put her through?

He swallowed back the guilt, lifted his hand and knocked. Grace ushered him in, stripping him of his wet coat, and handed him a cup of hot coffee.

"Get Mr. Pickett a blanket, Henry," she said to her husband, her brogue thick making the word "get" sound like "git."

Henry Mackenzie thumbed over his shoulder toward the closed door. "They're all in there."

Sam knew instantly that Kate was behind that door.

"Oh, for heaven's sakes," came the reply from his wife.

"Well, then, you go get it."

Grace marched toward the door and then changed her mind and stopped before Sam. Her voice now had none of the irritation she had shown with her husband.

"She was upset, so we gave her some privacy. I cleaned

the dirt and gravel out of her hand. Just scraped is all and I'm heating some water to soak her feet. Why don't you go in and comfort her?"

Sam hesitated, feeling suddenly cold inside and out. He hadn't tried to comfort anyone since his mother had left them at the orphanage. *Don't cry, Randy. I'll take care of you.*

He reached for the latch but paused at the unfamiliar sound. He pressed his ear to the rough boards. She was crying.

Sam backed away from the door. He had no idea how to console a weeping woman. It wasn't the type of skill he had developed from his early childhood in a whorehouse or later with the nuns.

Besides, it was his damn fault she was crying in the first place.

Grace gave him a nudge. "Go on, lad. She won't bite you."

When he still hesitated, she reached around him and rapped on the door.

"Sam's here, miss."

The door flew open and Kate flung herself into his arms. He glanced back at the couple to find Grace standing misty-eyed with her hands clasped at her bosom. Her husband, on the other hand, seemed to have taken a sudden interest in the ceiling planking.

"Come, Gracie." Henry grasped her arm and drew her toward the door. "Call if you need us." He hurried his wife from the cabin.

"Oh, Sam. I'm so sorry about John. It's all my fault. I couldn't run fast enough," said Kate.

"Man's a hero."

"What if he died because of me? I couldn't live with that."

He held her tight. "We're searching now. We'll find him."

She wrapped her arms about him and the rough wool blanket dropped from her shoulders onto the floor. She still stood in her muddy clothing.

"Come on, Kate. We need to get out of these duds."

He searched the bedroom and found Kate a flannel robe and nightgown, which she refused to put on until she had washed. He inspected her hands and found them the only clean part of her. The scrapes had already stopped bleeding.

Nothing from the foreman's small wardrobe would fit Sam, so he called out to his guards.

"Get me something to wear."

One of the men headed off.

Sam stripped out of his wet things and wrapped the blanket around his waist. Then he filled the tin washtub for Kate.

"Right here in the middle of the kitchen?" she asked, sounding horrified.

"I'll guard the door."

She lowered her chin and stared at him. "I'm not worried about who's outside."

He folded his arms over his chest. "I think I can contain myself until you're clean and dressed."

But it turned out he couldn't. He had to help her out of her tattered jacket, peeling it off like the skin of an orange. Then he pulled the ruffled blouse over her head.

That left her in a nearly transparent chemise and a corset that pressed her breasts invitingly up at him. He gulped.

"I knew it," she said.

He walked to the door and pressed his head to the solid wood. "Just wash up quick, will you?"

A few moments later he heard the splashing. Facing the door didn't help. It just allowed his mind to supply images of Kate naked and as slick as a seal.

He turned around and found that his mind did not do her justice, for his imaginings were nothing compared with the picture she made standing naked in the tub all rosy and wet.

He took a step in her direction. A knock sounded at the door. Kate leaped out of the water and grabbed the quilt he had left her.

Sam opened the door. Instead of the clothing he expected he found a rider standing before him, still gripping the reins of his lathered horse. He glanced at the beast's heaving sides and the foam dripping from its mouth.

"What's happened?" asked Sam.

"We found him, Mr. Pickett. Potts. He was clinging to a logjam."

Kate flew to the door, elbowing past Sam. Her borrowed robe was cinched, but her calves and ankles were bare.

"Is he alive?"

The man stumbled back a step as he gazed in astonishment at Kate, wet hair tumbling down her back and bosom heaving.

"Ah…"

Sam scowled, wrapping an arm around Kate's waist, drawing her back to him. "Spit it out, man."

"Yes. Alive."

"Injured?" he asked.

"Doesn't appear to be. Just shivering like a…" He glanced at Kate and lost the ability to speak once more. Sam was beginning to get used to the effect she had on men. He understood the rider's befuddlement as he found himself in the same state much of the time.

"Where is he?"

"They're bringing him to the camp now."

Sam nodded. "See to his needs and we'll speak to him tomorrow. Call me if there's any change."

The rider nodded and backed off the porch.

"Thank you," called Kate.

The man cleared his throat, but his voice still cracked when he spoke to her. "You're welcome."

Sam closed the door in his face.

"Are you trying to torture the man?"

"What do you mean?"

"You haven't got a stitch on under that robe and you're still cold." He stared at her chest.

"Oh!" She flushed, folding her arms across her chest.

"Too late now. Lucky he didn't take a fit right there on the threshold."

"I was just so relieved. Oh, Sam! He's alive! I'm so happy. My prayers were answered."

He scowled. The bad things he'd prayed wouldn't happen had all happened anyway, leaving him to try and live with them. Some days were easier than others.

"Sam?" She stared at him with open curiosity. "Are you all right?"

"Not for a long time." He peered out the window. "Where are my damned clothes?"

Kate stepped forward and rested her hands on his bare chest. "Do you really need them?"

He drew her in, relishing the clean, soapy scent of her skin. He breathed deep, cradling her head in the palm of his hand. She stared up at him with green eyes that promised him the world.

"I thought I'd lost you today," he whispered. "Never want to feel like that again."

She stroked his back with her fingertips, encouraging him.

"Kate, I realized something out there."

She smiled up at him. All the anxiety had gone out of her now. Her conscience was clear and her heart glad.

"I don't want to lose you."

"You didn't, silly." She tried to wiggle back into his arms.

He held her back. "You don't understand. When that dam broke, something changed inside me."

Her forehead wrinkled now. "Sam, what are you saying?"

How could he tell her he wanted more than just a few nights' pleasure. That he wanted her in the morning, afternoon and evening from now until he saw his last sunset. He wanted to share his dreams and his nightmares and to offer her his heart.

He wanted her to be his wife.

Don't mention marriage. That would surely send her running.

"You're not going back to your aunt's house. I want you to stay with me."

"Yes, Sam. We agreed on that already. An apartment, wardrobe—"

"I'm not talking about our arrangement." His voice was sharper than he intended.

He felt her stiffen and edge back. He clamped his teeth together to keep from mentioning what he really wanted. She'd only known him a few days. It was too soon to have fallen in love with him, wasn't it? Yet he was absolutely certain that Kate was the woman for him. Nothing on earth had ever felt so right as this.

If only he could convince her to take a chance on him. If she'd only do that, he'd spend his life trying to make her happy.

"Sam?"

He stared down at her, wanting her, needing her and still fearing that she would reject him.

She pressed herself against his chest. "I'm cold, Sam."

He gathered her close. This much, at least, she would accept from him. It showed she no longer feared him, didn't it?

It was a beginning.

He swept her into his arms and carried her into the bedroom.

Chapter Seventeen

An hour later, Kate gazed at the stripped pine beams crossing the ceiling. The fading sunlight made the room golden and cozy. She snuggled beneath the patch quilt that covered them after their lovemaking and wished this was her home.

How lovely it would be if Sam was not the richest man in Sacramento and she was not his mistress. She imagined trading places with the foreman and his wife. He would see to the mill and she would care for their home.

In her fantasy, she was free of the responsibility of her aging aunt, the boardinghouse and her sister.

Kate squeezed her eyes shut tight as the shame surged through her. How could she want to abandon Phoebe even in a silly fantasy, when Phoebe's condition was entirely her fault? Kate knew she could never make that right, but she could make her sister's life bearable. But now she had gotten all tangled up inside. Now she was envisioning things that would never happen and overlooking things she could never forsake.

She had expected to be crushed beneath Sam's boot heel. How could she have anticipated that he would treat her with kindness and dignity or that she would long for him with her body and soul?

He was remarkable. In mere days, he had changed her opinion on so many things. And she no longer dreaded his touch, in fact, she longed for it.

She stroked Sam's arm. Sam startled awake, glanced at her, smiled and fell back to the bed. Perhaps he was no more used to sharing a bed than she was. Kate dragged the quilt up over his shoulder.

"You warmed up now?" he muttered.

"Yes, thank you."

He grunted. "Good, 'cause you're likely to kill me if we do that again."

She laughed. "I am sorry to be such a burden."

He squeezed her tight. "'S all right."

His eyes closed again and he rested his chin on the top of her head.

He gripped her bottom and drew her close. "I wouldn't mind being wrapped up like this every night."

It wasn't a future exactly, but did cause the slightest twinkle of hope, as if the evening star had just appeared in the night sky for her to wish upon. Perhaps he would not grow tired of her *too* quickly.

"I don't think I've ever been that cold before," she said, nestling close.

He stiffened. "I have."

Something about the way he said that sent a chill

down her spine. His voice had sounded strained. She drew back to look at Sam but what she saw gave her no reassurance. He stared off at nothing as he clenched and unclenched his jaw. The hand that a moment earlier had caressed her shoulder now bunched into a trembling fist. Her heart began to thud painfully in her chest.

"Sam?"

He didn't answer, as if he could not hear her.

She jostled him, pushing at his ribs. "Sam!"

He seemed to snap back to her and he blinked as if she had suddenly appeared from nowhere.

"What just happened?" she asked.

He pressed both hands over his eyes and gasped as if surfacing from deep water.

She rested a hand on his chest. He grasped it, holding her a little too tightly. It reminded her of the grip she'd had on his collar when she thought he would sink below the muddy water once more.

"Sam, tell me what's wrong."

He swallowed hard. "I want to. I just can't seem to find the words."

She sat up, tucking the quilt beneath her arms. "Sam, you're frightening me."

He pushed himself up beside her and rubbed his forehead. "Today you were worried about Mr. Potts."

"Yes. Because I felt responsible. He most certainly would have escaped harm if not for my slowing him."

"You were weighted down by guilt."

"That is it exactly." He understood then. Earlier she feared he might have misinterpreted her concern as some silly infatuation. Potts was very sweet and brave, but she had no feelings for him beyond profound gratitude and responsibility for his present situation.

"Then perhaps you can imagine what it might be like to carry that burden over the course of years rather than hours."

She tried to do as he asked and for some reason pictured an ember, burning into a piece of wood long after the flame had been extinguished. What burden did he carry? Was it hot like burning coal or cold like a shard of ice?

He stared down at her, his face earnest. "I've done something that tainted me. I don't ever feel clean since that day on the mountain."

Kate's body went cold as she recognized he was telling her about the Broadner Party.

His eyes looked sad. "I don't claim to understand what makes two people the same inside, Kate. But I know it when I see it. You've got starch in your spine. You're a fighter, like me. And you suffered your losses, things that would kill some folks. But they didn't kill us. You feel responsible for your sister's condition. While I've done something shameful and I can't forgive myself for it."

Kate felt a creeping dread as she wondered what he had done.

"I never told anyone about that time, but I think of it every damn day."

She cautioned herself not to be horrified by whatever he said. This was Sam and she trusted him. Whatever it was, she was sure he'd had no choice.

"Me and Cole were mule skinners on the journey

west, driving the teams. I'd just started shaving at the start. When we reached these here mountains, the snows came early, the families broke up to make their own shelters. But we had no families, so they left me and Cole high and dry. See we didn't have no supplies of our own as we was working our way across. The deal included food and a spot under the wagon, but all bets were off after that snow."

Kate clenched her fists about the quilt, drawing it up to her mouth, afraid of what he would say next. He must have seen her tension, for he rested his hand over hers, patting it gently as if to comfort her.

"Cole and I had little choice but to go. We formed a party of those without means, and some of the mothers with small children, desperate to get help. Cole was in a worse fix than me, because he had a wife and young daughter. My boss and his wife agreed to care for Lee-lee, so Angela, that was Cole's wife, left the child and we set out." His eyes took on a faraway look, as if he were no longer there in the bedroom with her but off on the mountain seeing it all over again. As the daylight faded, he told her how they had used oxbows to make snowshoes and how the men broke trail. How some grew exhausted and were left behind. How freezing rains had separated their party and how he had elected to stay back when his friend's wife took sick.

"We ran out of food and Angela took a real high fever. She didn't know what was happening much of the time, which was a blessing. But at the end she was clear in her mind. Last thing she said to Cole was, 'Promise me you'll get help for Lee-lee.' And I heard him promise. But after she passed, he wouldn't get up. He just lay there in the snow beside his wife. That's when they came back."

He stopped the telling. She met his troubled gaze.

"Who came back?" she whispered in the gathering dark.

Sam's expression went hard as he stared past her at the wall. "The Devlins—Charles, Amelia and their two grown sons. They was the family Cole worked for. At first I thought they'd come to help, but there aren't words to describe what they wanted."

She held her breath. She'd heard grim tales of the survivors left in camp. She knew what the deprivation had wreaked there. But there had been no stories from the survivors who walked out. Sam's expression echoed the horrors he had witnessed.

"They wanted her body. Said her sacrifice would save us all. That got Cole on his feet in a hurry. He drew his pistol and drove them off. They made like they was going but only so we wouldn't see Devlin draw. Cole had holstered his weapon but Devlin's shot missed. Cole's didn't—shot Devlin right between the eyes. He told his widow if they were hungry they could eat that. We watched them drag off the body. I helped Cole bury his wife. He wanted to wrap Angela in my blanket, but I wouldn't give it to him. I knew that blanket was all that kept us alive the first two nights. The ground was frozen, of course, so we used branches and rocks and such, trying to build a grave to keep the scavengers off her body. It took nearly all our energy. We was so weak, you see, from the hunger and cold. When we was finished, Cole decided maybe he'd stay right there. I reminded him of his promise. Lee-lee was waitin' for her papa. That got him walking again. It wasn't long after that that we found Devlin's body. His family had stripped the flesh off the back of his legs and left him right out in the open like a butchered hog."

Sam glanced down at Kate and she knew without him speaking what he had done. Her eyes widened and he swallowed before confirming what she already knew.

"Cole never touched that body. I wish to God I could say the same. I'm damned for it now."

Kate choked back her abhorrence, the overwhelming revulsion at what he had done. But he must have seen it, for he inhaled sharply and drew back. She let him go, at a loss now for what to say.

"It's why I don't speak of it. That look you gave me. It's disgust. It *is* disgusting. I know it. You can't do such a thing and not be fouled by it."

The repugnance receded, replaced by an overwhelming sense of empathy. He looked so shattered by her reaction. It shamed her. "No, that's not true. But Sam, it's horrible. What you must have suffered. I'm so terribly sorry."

His brow wrinkled. "Sorry?"

"Oh, yes. It must be a hard thing to reconcile."

"It can't be. And I can't live with it, either. I'd do anything to go back to that moment."

"But what choice did you have but death?"

She brushed the hair back from his temple and he

allowed it. Then she crawled upward until she could bring his head to rest upon her bare breast. She stroked him, dragging her fingers rhythmically through his hair and felt the hot splash of his tears on her skin.

"You saved his life, Sam. Cole never would have made it out without you."

"I did it to save myself. I did it because the hunger was like a madness. What other explanation is there for doing such an evil thing?"

"Survival, Sam. We all do what we must to live."

"I don't understand why I survived when so many good decent folks died."

"You lived because you were stronger and because you were brave enough to do things weaker men couldn't stomach."

"Selfish, you mean."

"You made it out. You told the outside world that there was a wagon train stranded in the pass. All who were rescued owe you their lives."

"They didn't all survive," he said.

She kissed his troubled brow. "They didn't all die, either."

"I haven't been up here since. Too many ghosts."

"Sam?"

He drew away and sat beside her. "I understand, Kate, if you don't want any part of me. I wouldn't blame you, either."

She held his hand. "I think you're a hero and the most noble man I have ever met."

He stared at her. His expression radiated astonishment that dissolved into gratitude.

"I never expected you to say nothing like that," he whispered. "I figured you'd want no more to do with me after you knew."

"Guess you figured wrong."

Another piece of the puzzle that was Sam suddenly slipped neatly into place. "That's why you want to close the pass. Why you are building the railroad."

"Once she's built, nobody else will ever have to face early snows again. I've sunk my last dollar into that project and convinced lots of folks to do the same. I thought if I did this, maybe the ghosts wouldn't bother me so much. Maybe I'd find some peace or at least have one thing I could be proud of."

She gaped at him. "One thing? Sam, you hit one of the biggest strikes of gold in California."

"Kate, my own mother didn't want me. You think gold can fill that hole?"

She felt her heart breaking for him.

"I need that railroad. Nobody's going to stop me. Not Donahue or all the shippers in San Francisco."

Kate thought of something then, something she hadn't understood this morning—was it only this morning? It seemed like a lifetime ago. She recalled the gift he had presented. The meaning that had escaped her now became crystal clear.

"Sam, the railroad stock—you gave me a piece of your dream, didn't you?"

He smiled and made the slightest nod.

"Thank you for sharing this with me."

He toyed with a strand of her hair, winding it around

his finger. "I thought it would sicken you, what I done up here in these mountains."

"You misjudged me."

The hardest part was telling the boarders that she was closing the house. Ella Maguire gave them the same amount of notice that the bank gave her—one week.

The sale of the piano gave her enough ready cash to rent a one-bedroom apartment and to hire a boy to move their personal belongings in. Kate would be so disappointed that she had failed to sell the necklace. Not just failed, but somehow managed to cast a shadow of suspicion on her niece. That terrible woman had spun a web of lies as masterfully as any weaver.

"Will Kate be able to find us?" asked Phoebe.

Ella tucked her niece against her side. "Of course she will. I've left word with the neighbors."

And the police had Ella's new address in case they needed to speak to her again. That thought turned her stomach to ice. What had Kate gotten involved in?

She trusted Kate. But she did have a reckless side. It explained her first marriage and her acceptance of the very improper offer by Mr. Pickett.

But Kate would never have become involved in a scheme to defraud Mr. Pickett. She'd stake her life on it.

Chapter Eighteen

Kate's stomach growled so loudly that Sam jumped.

"Holy mackerel, we best get you fed." He slid from the bed and got two oil lamps lit. He returned with one and set it beside the bed. He pressed his hands to his bare hips. "Didn't I tell someone to get me some proper clothing?"

Kate rose, relinquishing the quilt so Sam would have something to cover himself as he went to the door. She stared down at her hands, tipping them toward the lamplight. The cut on her right index finger gapped when she pinched it, but the rest were scabbing up nicely.

Sam returned a moment later with a stack of neatly folded clothing and a covered crock.

As Sam changed, Kate slipped into the nightgown and robe and investigated the crock and found a fine-looking beef stew that had congealed. However, the foreman's wife kept an orderly home and the stove fires were nicely banked. Kate had little trouble stoking them. By the time Sam emerged from the bedroom, she had added kindling and was placing their meal on the burner to warm.

He came up behind her, resting his hands on her hips. It stirred bad memories of Luke, but rather than stiffen, she leaned back against him, replacing the bad with good.

Sam enfolded her in his arms and nuzzled her neck.

She clasped his arms, now looped about her waist, and rocked slightly back and forth with him in a silent dance of comfort and contentment.

"If you don't let go of me, we'll both starve to death."

He squeezed her tight. "I'll never let go."

Kate sighed, trying to remember that it was only teasing, only words. But her heart believed him—or wanted to believe him. It was her mind that resisted, knowing how much more painful their parting would be if she was foolish enough to fall in love with him.

He stepped away, but gave her backside a little pat. She turned and caught sight of his wardrobe for the first time. He wore a red flannel shirt, rolled at the sleeves as if he meant to go out and split cordwood. He looked fully capable, with his broad chest and well-muscled arms. He also wore a pair of jeans that fit him remarkably well and his feet were now covered with gray wool socks. She blinked at him, thinking how natural he looked in the clothing of a laborer. It seemed to suit him better than his finely tailored garments. It only reinforced the illusion that he was an ordinary man instead of someone of importance. She wished he was a laborer and she wished he was hers.

"You look ready to work at the mill." She could not

resist stroking the red flannel of his sleeve as she admired him. "Those clothes fit you so well."

"They ought to. They're mine."

"Yours!"

"I keep some things up here." He stood awkwardly now, waiting, but for what she did not know.

"Well, they're very handsome."

He grinned. "I used to dress like this every day. But then I made a fortune and everyone said I should put my dungarees away." He stroked the faded old denim. "I miss them."

She folded her arms before her and studied him a moment. "Yes, they suit you."

He reached for her and she thrust two ceramic bowls at him.

"Find us some spoons."

He did and a few moments later they were enjoying a meal together with none of the awkward tension of the last time they dined.

Kate remembered something. "Oh, Sam, thank you for sending the tea."

He paused and smiled at her. "I'm trying to please you, Kate, in everything. I'm just still so new at this. Never spent this much time with a woman before. But you make it easy."

"Most of the time, you mean."

They shared a friendly smile as if they had done this many times before. He emptied his bowl and she rose to refill it.

"Much as I'd like to keep you in night clothing, I guess I better see about getting your things sent up here."

She set a second helping before him.

"I'm going to check on the rail workers farther up the mountain tomorrow and I want you along."

"You want to show me off again?" she asked, trying to keep her smile from slipping.

He stared at her in silence for a moment. "No one up there to impress. It's just my Chinese workers laying track and the Welsh laying charges, trying to bust a hole through the mountain for a tunnel. I imagine seeing you would be a welcome relief. Likely it'd be safer to leave you here till I get back, but I like having you around. Besides, I gotta keep you from climbing any more trees and shredding the rest of the duds I bought you."

He didn't want to display her. She felt ashamed at her assumption. "I'm sorry about the lovely habit. It's such a pity."

"Think your petticoats have reached the American River yet?"

That thought made her blush and then laugh out loud.

"I could get used to that sound," he said accepting the second helping.

Kate took her place across from him and wished she could stop time and stay here in this tiny cabin, for she could not recall another moment when she had ever been as happy as she was right now.

Early the following morning the illusion of domestic bliss shattered with a persistent knocking at the door.

Sam answered the summons, then dressed, kissed her and disappeared before Kate could crawl out of bed and drag on her borrowed robe. Where he got the energy, she could not fathom.

Sam had abandoned her to see about the dam's reconstruction, the cartographer's safety and she could not recall what all.

The enormity of the logistical details of such a massive project quite boggled her, but Sam seemed to feed off the energy he expended and, like a Yule log, only burned more brightly.

Kate's muscles ached today. She groaned as she lifted the heavy pitcher. Washing her face was a task because the soap and water stung the abrasions on her palms. But all in all, she felt lucky to be in one piece.

Kate's clothing arrived with her breakfast. Kate was again faced with a lumberjack's meal, fully cooked and somewhat cold. The massive portion was accompanied with a piping hot pot of coffee. Kate tried not to let the setback dampen her enthusiasm. Sam was taking her to the track's end to see the construction of the railroad.

She was pleased to hear that Mr. Potts had resumed his duties and was personally seeing to their transport back down to the railroad. From there she would ride to nearly the last laid rail at the terminus some thirty miles east of Dutch Flats.

As Kate finished what she could of the meal, Grace Mackenzie arrived. With her assistance, Kate dressed in a flamboyant day dress.

"Never seen anyone wear more than three petticoats and that's in the winter," she observed, but laced the seven that Kate insisted on.

The dress itself was a lovely cocoa-colored satin that

shone with silver highlights in the sunshine. She wore brown kid slippers this day, as she would not be walking, riding or climbing trees.

By midday, she discovered that the foreman's wife had a teapot and tin of black tea. The water was heated and poured over he dry leaves. The aroma filled Kate with anticipation. She had just sat down to wait for the leaves to steep when Sam arrived.

"The wagon's ready and Potts is driving you."

Kate gasped in surprise and rose to her feet. Her savior had arrived.

Sam's smile dropped away as his gaze swept her. "Tarnation, look at you." He extended his hand and she accepted it. He turned her this way and that. "You're as shiny as a minnow."

She laughed. "Such a flatterer. I won't be climbing any trees today, will I?"

He chuckled and offered his elbow. "Not planning on it, but you never can tell. I do love those bloomers."

She leaned close and whispered. "Then why did you order me to abandon them our first night together?"

He chuckled and led her out. "Guess I like what's underneath better."

His bawdy comment should have made her blush, but instead she squeezed his arm in delight, happy that he wanted her. Happy to be at his side.

"Ready?" he asked.

She spared one longing glance at her untouched tea, but she could certainly forgo this to thank the man responsible for saving her life.

"Sam, would you do something for me?"

He nodded, without asking what that something might be.

"Will you reward Mr. Potts in some way for the risk he took?"

"I've promoted him, given him shares in the company and fired every bastard who ran."

Kate could only blink in shock. With all he had to do, he had managed that quite neatly.

Kate drew on her gloves and recovered her hat.

He offered his arm.

A moment later she abandoned him to hug John Potts. Her embrace completely flummoxed the man, dissolving him into a red-faced, stammering fool.

"Take a breath, son," said Sam.

Kate stood back, waiting. When Mr. Potts seemed to be breathing again, she thanked him.

"Oh, it was nothing much."

"You are as modest as you are brave."

Sam helped her up in the wagon as John climbed to the opposite side. Sam motioned and four armed riders flanked the wagon.

"Aren't you coming?" she asked.

"I've got to meet the cartographers later on and there's no wagon road up there, so you're going back to the train for now."

Her disappointment showed on her face, but she said nothing to this. A mistress awaited her consort, not the other way around. She had absolutely no grounds to be cross.

He took her hand and lowered his voice. His smile was pure promise. "I'll be there after dark."

"Of course. Shall I wait supper for you?"

"Naw. I'll be late."

She leaned down and kissed his cheek. He waved to the riders and the small regiment pulled out. The journey was uneventful, but it was shocking to see all the damage the water had done to the road and the meadow below. The lovely wildflowers were flattened and the large boulders that had filled the stream had completely disappeared.

"It hardly looks like the same place," she said to Mr. Potts.

He nodded. "That's a fact."

"I can never thank you enough for what you did for me."

"Only did as I was told. Mr. Pickett left you in my care. I don't take that lightly."

"You're a good friend."

His smile was nearly imperceptible. "I try."

She shivered at the memory of yesterday.

"Which tree do you think it was?"

"Passed it a while back. I notched it so as I could find it again. Mr. Pickett sent me for a piece of wood off it for whittling."

She grinned at this.

"I wasn't suppose to say, was I?"

"He mentioned it to me. Is he a good whittler?"

"Fair."

She wondered what he would fashion from the wood.

They reached the train without trouble and she spoke to Sam's cook, pleading for tea. The burly fellow scratched his head and then promised he'd see about getting some.

Instead, he surprised her at lunch with a warm cup of cocoa. She didn't have the heart to tell him she was disappointed and as a result got cocoa again at supper.

As she sat alone in the posh comfort of the compartment, she tried to recall the last time she had dined alone. The boarding house was always a bustling, lively place. Now she sat in luxury and solitude like a pet parrot. She stared out into the darkness beyond the window and thought of Phoebe, wondering how her sister was getting on without her there.

Cole Ellis arrived at two in the afternoon, riding a lathered horse. Sam met his partner in front of the mill.

"So you caught one of them," said Cole, responding to the message Sam had sent him yesterday.

"Yeah, but he died."

Cole dismounted. "Did they damage the mill?"

"No, but without the dam we can't turn the wheel. I've got three shifts working the crosscut saws, but we can't keep up with the demand."

"We'll have to ship them in, then."

"You tell Crawford about Donahue?"

"He's on it. Got his people in San Francisco contacting the police."

"Police! Donahue owns half the damn force, plus keeps a private army of deputies."

"That what you call them—deputies? Thugs, you mean. Anyway, Crawford says we still have to file charges, in case anything else happens."

Sam snorted. "Fat lot of good that will do."

"Hey, you hired him."

"I thought you hired him."

Cole grinned. "Maybe I did."

Sam did not feel jovial after seeing his dam wash downstream. "I'm afraid to send men out of camp unless they're well armed and in groups."

"That's wise."

Sam flagged down one of his men and sent him for food, then he led Cole to the mill which was uncharacteristically silent. All the belts and wheels sat still in the empty room.

"I got coffee on the stove," said Sam.

Cole poured a cup and took a swallow. "Tastes good."

The men sat in matching ladder-back chairs before the potbellied stove with their tin cups of black coffee.

"Where's the beauty?" asked Cole.

"Her name's Kate and I sent her back to the railcars under guard until I know it's safe."

"Kate, huh? Seems too informal for her, too—I don't know—ordinary, I guess. Katherine, maybe suits her better."

"You didn't see her climb a tree yesterday."

Cole lowered the coffee and stared, disbelief evident in his expression.

"Never been so scared. She was below the dam when it blew."

"Never?" The two men exchanged looks. Sam knew what Cole was thinking. The two of them on the mountain, freezing, starving and dying.

"It's different being afraid for someone else." He likely shouldn't have said that as it would get Cole thinking about Angela.

His friend simply nodded his agreement, his face solemn. "Like that, is it? You falling in love with her?"

Sam nodded. "Maybe so."

Cole winced. "You've only known her a few days."

He let his irritation spill over. "What's that got to do with it?"

"Sam, you've avoided this for as long as I've known you. Give me a minute to get used to the idea, is all."

"I've avoided it because I got no experience."

Cole laughed. "You've got more experience than any man I know."

"Not with bedding them!"

Cole's smile faded. "You talking about marriage?"

"Maybe." Sam shook his head and glanced back to Cole.

"Big step. Best be sure, first."

"I am sure, sure that I'll screw it up. I ain't got a notion how to make a home for her with suppertime and kids and flowers in vases." He kicked the leg of the stove.

"And you want that kind of life?"

"I'd rather face an earthquake in a mine shaft."

Cole leveled a cool eye on Sam, not letting him dodge the question. "Not what I asked you."

Sam pressed his lips together, scowled at his friend and admitted his yearnings aloud. "Yes, damn it. I want it."

Sam glared at Cole. "But not everyone can have what you got, you know?"

"What?"

"A family."

"No, but I think *you* can." Cole gave him a long look. "She has a reputation."

"So do I."

"Hers might make you look like the prize-winning goat at the fair. She married money before."

Sam met Cole's look of concern with a cold stare. Only their long friendship kept him from taking a swing at him.

"Cole, we both know that I've done a lot worse than marry for money, so don't even think she ain't good enough for me."

"You have no cause to apologize."

Sam snorted.

"You know," said Cole. "It's the women who make houses into homes. Kate will know what to do."

"Except she's already got a home and she told me outright that she wasn't interested in marrying again. Not that I blame her."

Cole sat forward, cradling his half-finished coffee in his hands between his legs. "Why's that?"

"You remember her first husband?"

"He got exactly what he deserved."

"He mistreated her, Cole. He hurt her bad."

Cole's expression turned stormy. "Reason enough to be wary of marriage, bad experience like that."

Sam picked a blade of grass off the heel of his boot and rolled it between his thumb and forefinger. "I'm afraid I remind her of that bastard."

"You're not like him. She must see that."

"Ain't I? We both made a fortune. We both can't get enough of her. And, apparently, we both spend a good deal of time ordering her around."

"She's gun-shy. She'll come around."

"Her opinion of marriage ain't changed because of me. She sees it as some kind of jail sentence."

"Last time we spoke, you felt much the same."

Sam dropped the grass blade and stared at Cole. "I never had nothing against it. I just can't see it working out, but I can't seem to walk away, neither."

"You need to give her some time to get to know you. If you two share this feeling, she'll want to stay. But let her get used to the idea or you'll scare her off."

Sam cradled his forehead in his palm.

"I've seen you take some chances that took real guts. Maybe this is no different."

"Feels different."

Cole's smile seemed wise. "That's good."

"Then why do I want to punch something?"

Cole laughed. "If you love her, Sam, you can't do anything else but take the gamble, because not being with her will scare you more than taking a chance."

Chapter Nineteen

Kate woke at the low vibration, causing the bed to shudder. It took a moment to recall her surroundings. She was thankful she left one of the wall lamps burning low.

Sam had not returned—had he?

She peered about and recognized the engine's low rumble. The train was readying for departure.

"Sam?"

The room was empty. She went to the window and peeked beneath the blind but saw only darkness. Kate pulled on her robe but did not tie it.

The train would not leave without Sam. That meant he was aboard. She hurried into her slippers and headed for the next car, certain she would find him there and if not, she would await him. Yes, he'd like that.

The door slid open and she paused in the chilly night air, then hurried between the cars, bursting into the next room.

"Sam?" She came through the narrow hall past the necessary and stepped out into the main room where her hurried step screeched to a halt.

There sat Sam, smoking a cigar beside the man she'd met at the station, his partner. The man bolted to his feet at her entrance looking as shocked as if a grizzly bear had charged into the coach.

Kate gasped at his wide-eyed sweep of her dishabille. She drew the edges of the robe together too late, for he had already seen much of her charms through the sheer lace gown. Why hadn't it occurred to her that someone else might be with him?

Because she'd been so anxious to see Sam, nothing else crossed her mind.

"Oh, Katie, sweetheart. I'll be along in a few minutes," said Sam.

Kate's cheeks burned as she backed up, her arms clamped before her.

"I'm sorry," she whispered, turned and fled. She reached the bed and sank into the mattress, wishing she could disappear. She pressed her scabby palms to her burning face. How could she be so stupid?

A mistress waited in bed for her benefactor. She didn't go dancing about half-naked before his partner. What would he do when he came in?

Luke would have been furious. She straightened as if soaked in ice water and then began to shake.

"He's not Luke," she whispered, praying that she was right. But the fear gnawed at her, filling her mind with doubt.

* * *

Cole sank back to his seat with a low whistle. Then he looked at Sam.

Sam pointed a finger at him. "Don't say anything that I'll have to kill you over."

Cole shook his head, indicating he wouldn't, and now seemed unable to say anything.

"Well?" said Sam.

"You're a lucky man."

Sam scowled.

"If you don't marry her, you're a fool."

"You don't marry a woman because she looks fetching in white lace."

"Seems reason enough right now."

Sam rose. "See you in the morning."

Cole followed Sam to his feet. "I'll tell the engineer you're ready to roll and see about ordering up those rail ties."

Sam walked him to the door.

"I need you to make a stop at a jewelry store."

Cole made a face.

Sam swallowed, knowing Cole would tease him, but felt this was right.

"Buy an engagement ring for me?"

"I'm already married." His friend didn't even crack a smile. "Besides, that's something a man should pick out for himself."

"Just buy the biggest damn one you can find."

"Okay, partner."

Cole shook his hand and headed out.

* * *

Sam opened the door to the sleep compartment and found the room as quiet as a crypt. She could not possibly have fallen asleep so fast. He crept toward the bed and found her lying on her back, her head turned to the side and her eyes closed.

Golden lamplight gilded her hair and skin. Her slim arm rested on top of the coverlet. Her unnatural stillness concerned him for a moment until he realized the game. She was pretending to be asleep.

He sat on the bed, leaning over her to rest one hand on either side of her shoulders.

"Kate, I know you're awake."

She blinked her eyes open and stared up at him. Was she clenching her jaw?

"Kate?" He couldn't keep the concern from his voice. "I'm sorry I left you alone all day. Are you all right?"

The tears came so fast it was like seeing the dam break all over again. Only this time, instead of hitting him in the gut, the flood hit him straight in the heart.

He gathered her up. "What's wrong, honey?"

Her words came fast, frantic and edged with panic. "I'm sorry. I didn't know you had company. I embarrassed you. Please forgive me, Sam."

He held her at arm's length so he could look at her. What was going on?

"I like to show you off, Katie. Just not quite so much of you all at once."

She buried her face in her hands.

"That's my friend, Cole. You met him, remember? He's been my partner. We crossed the country together."

She made a whimpering sound.

"He don't mind. He's got a wife and all. Nothing he ain't seen before, I'd imagine."

She blinked up at him, sending more tears cascading down her lovely face. "You forgive me?"

"Anything."

She drew a breath, clasping her hands before her bosom. This caused her charms to swell to near bursting. Sam's eyes bugged and he tried to recall that he strove to comfort her. Damn all that lace.

She lunged at him, throwing herself into his arms and pressing her wonderful bosom tight to his chest.

He closed his eyes and enfolded her in his embrace.

He could read a trace vein of quartz and follow it to gold like a bloodhound after spoor. But to read the signals a woman sent seemed near impossible.

She drew back and he had to force himself to release her.

Kate was all smiles now and gladness.

"Kate? What just happened?"

"Nothing. I was certain you'd be furious at me for my mistake."

Sam thought a moment and suddenly it made sense. The feigned sleep, the fear in her eyes.

"This is about him, again, isn't it?"

Now she looked worried. She was right, this time. No man wanted to be constantly reminded of another lover. He scowled and she inched away. It occurred to him that she was struggling to read him in the same way he labored to understand her.

"It's all right, Kate. I wasn't mad about what happened

earlier and I'm not mad now. But you got to judge me on what I do, not on what that bastard would have done."

She nodded solemnly and then graced him with a tentative smile. "I missed you."

He grinned at her. "How much?"

She flipped back the coverlet.

The railcar jumped.

Kate gripped the blankets. "What was that?"

"Decoupling our cars. Cole's taking the rest back down for lumber." And an engagement ring. "He'll be back in the morning and we'll continue up the line."

"Oh." She released her death grip on the bedding. "So we're alone?"

"Except for the Pinkertons surrounding the cars. You're safe."

Kate's smile was full of promise. "Not too safe, I hope."

Sam felt a rush of heat that had nothing to do with the cozy bed and everything to do with the warm, willing woman sheathed in sheer lace.

He had his boots and gun belt off a moment later, and then peeled down to his long johns which required unbuttoning. He sat on the bed and struggled with the buttons. Just when he decided to tear the fabric, he heard a giggle.

Kate knelt behind him on the bed, her warm fingers dancing over his neck to delve into the nest of curly hair covering his chest. When her fingertips brushed over his nipples, he sucked in a breath as if preparing to dive into deep water and pressed his back against her. Her clever fingers released the buttons of his underthings. She kissed his neck as she drew the cotton fabric over his shoulder, her hot mouth burning along the flesh she exposed. He groaned and she giggled again.

That was enough of this. He vowed that the next sound she made would be not a laugh but a tortured little cry of hunger. He dragged off the last remaining garment and kicked it clear across the room.

Then he turned toward her to find her still kneeling, the image of female perfection swathed in lace. He could see her rosy nipples through the gossamer gown and the dark thatch of hair at the juncture of her thighs. He clasped her hips, finding her skin warm and supple. From his position, seated on the edge of the bed, he found himself at eye level with her breasts. The flimsy nightgown was no barrier at all to his questing lips. When he took her nipple in his mouth, she gave a cry and fell forward, arching to offer herself to him. Now it was his turn to smile.

His hands slid under the gown, stroking up her soft thighs and then moving over the graceful swell of her buttocks. He was halted by the ribbons tying the front of her night rail. He left the sweet delight of her breast to clasp the troublesome ribbon in his teeth and pull until the bow released. The garment gaped and Sam's hands continued to stroke from her navel to the flat plain of her breastbone, kissing and licking his way along.

Kate arched over his arm as he revealed her torso. He dragged the nightgown from her body, leaving her naked in his arms. When she tried to lie back upon the bed he drew her close, bringing her before him as he sat on the edge of the bed. He slowly released his hold so she slid along him until her knees met his thighs. Just as she was about to straddle his legs, he stopped her, gripping her tight. Then he used one hand to stroke her lovely bottom and slide his fingers between the clefts of her backside. He growled his pleasure at discovering the wet, slick skin there. He tipped his head and smiled up at her. He used two fingers to slide inside her. She gasped, arching to allow him better access.

"Do you want me again, Kate?" he asked.

She nodded.

"As bad as I want you?"

She nodded again.

He drew his fingers out and held her a moment longer. Then he released his hold by slow degrees, allowing her to slide down his body until the tip of his erection grazed her wet folds. He stopped her again. She made a sound of frustration and tried to wiggle from his grasp.

He lifted his chin and she kissed him on his mouth with quick, eager thrusts of her tongue until he nearly lost his grip on her. She drew back.

"Let me have you," she whispered.

Her eagerness overtook him and he let her go. She moved down the length of him with a sigh of contentment and then settled her hips against him. She leaned back to press herself in more tightly, trusting him to keep her from falling. He held her as she swayed and then thrust his hips up to push deeper inside her.

She cried out and then used her strong legs to lift up, nearly unseating herself. She straightened and gazed down at him, watching his face as she slid over him again. He closed his eyes at the sweetness of her taking. Up she rose and then down again. He kissed her breasts and stroked her back as she rode him. She moved faster and he realized he was quickly losing control.

It was in that moment that he realized he didn't wear the French preventative. The second startling recognition was that he didn't want to.

He gripped her hips, stilling her. He held her sandwiched between one hand at her back and the other over her taut belly.

"Kate," he said, but did not know how to tell her.

Don't be a damned fool. Just because you want her child doesn't mean she wants it.

He drew her up and off until she stood on the carpet before him, looking confused. He grabbed at the drawer beside his bed and removed the paper packet. She took it with eager fingers. His head sank for a moment. She didn't want a child, then. If she did, she'd tell him no, wouldn't she?

She tore the packet open and slipped the skin over him. Then she climbed up over his hips, as bold as any wrangler, and seated herself back in place. He gasped as she took him, his thought blurring against the rising need.

His hand descended until his thumb brushed over the swollen bud between her legs. She gasped and shuddered. Her head fell back and her motion became more frantic. He increased the speed of his stroking and gritted his teeth, hoping he could hold back until she finished her ride.

She was close now. He could tell from the mewling sounds she made far back in her throat. But his release was coming and he did not know if he could wait. She arched and called out his name in a long cry of liberation. An instant later the rippling contractions of her release rolled over his erect flesh, splintering his control. He unlocked his jaw and gave in to pleasure that roared through him.

Chapter Twenty

Sam woke to a train whistle and knew Cole had returned with the lumber and, hopefully, the ring. But Sam did not rise as he felt the cars reconnect. Soon the engine was pushing them along to the building site. Only when the familiar rumble of steel wheels on the twin rails ceased and the train came to rest, did he rise. He found his partner at the cook's tent, beside the train, already drinking coffee.

"You look like hell," said Cole.

Sam knew a jealous man when he saw one. Cole never left Bridget for long. In the early days, they were inseparable, but now with the babies, she could not follow him so easily.

"I guess you got more sleep than I did," Sam said. "Did you get it?"

"What?" Cole didn't quite pull off the look of bewilderment, because he started laughing. "Yeah, I got it."

He reached in his trouser pocket and came up empty. "Must have lost it."

Sam folded his arms and waited.

Cole laughed again and then drew a small heart-shaped box from his vest pocket. It was red leather with a floral pattern embossed on the sides in gold.

"The box is sure pretty," said Sam.

"Well, I didn't pick it for the box. It isn't the biggest. But it was the best-looking one, I think. Still say you should have been the one to choose it."

"You got better taste for such things."

Sam used his thumb to flip open the lid. Inside, nestled in black velvet, sat the ring. It had a large white diamond in the center that sparkled when he tipped the box. The round stone was ringed with more white diamonds. More studded the sides of the band, although they were long and thin. The setting was silver and nearly invisible, making the ring seem all diamonds.

"You bought a silver ring?"

"That's platinum, you idiot."

"I'm an idiot? I'm not the man who bought a platinum ring for a gold miner's fiancée."

"If she don't like it, you can take it back. Besides I think the ring is the least of your worries."

"What's that supposed to mean?"

"Just that I've asked a woman to marry me and you haven't. Isn't as easy as you think."

Sam closed the box and tucked the ring away. "Thanks."

"Yeah." Cole glanced around. "Everything is good here? No more attacks and the supplies are all accounted for."

"I still want to speak to the head of each team."

"I'll see to that."

Sam nodded. "Appreciate that."

Cole rose and gulped down the rest of his coffee. Sam turned to the cook that he had had with him since the Dog Bite Mining Company.

"Lucky, I want a pot of Chinese tea in a teapot with sugar and milk, real milk." Sam scratched his chin. "Oh, and a fancy cup and spoon."

He turned back to see Cole smirking at him.

"That gonna hold you till lunch?"

"Climb off my back, will ya?"

Cole clapped him on the shoulder. "Just nice to see you taking care of someone, partner. Been a long time coming. Pardon me for enjoying myself."

Sam waved him off and headed back to Kate.

He found her struggling with her corset, so he helped cinch her in. It reminded him of saddling a horse, except that the horse held its breath to prevent him from tightening the girth, while Kate exhaled to expedite the procedure.

Once that ordeal was complete, he helped lift a black skirt above her head. As it settled over her hoop, he realized that the garment had alternating wide vertical stripes of shiny satin and soft velvet. Kate closed the velvet coat herself.

"Women's clothing makes no sense. What's the point of garments you can't get into by yourself?"

Kate finished fastening the jacket and turned to face him. The black made her skin seem pale as the sugar quartz in his mine. Her hair gleamed like burnished copper, looking rich and earthy beside the black. Suddenly he understood.

He smiled and nodded. "Worth every penny," he said. "I'm glad you approve."

Sam felt the ring burning a hole in his pocket. But he hadn't thought of what to say yet. Where was a man supposed to ask a woman? Certainly not in a bedroom with the rumpled sheets there as a reminder of the night they had spent together.

He'd wait until after they ate.

Sam held the door for her. Their breakfast was waiting for them in the adjoining car as he had instructed. He glanced over the lot and saw two covered trays and a silver coffeepot. How blessed difficult was it to find a cup of milk and a handful of dried tea leaves?

Kate took a seat and Sam drew the table between them, then lifted the closest lid. The first tray was obviously his, with a slab of ham as big around as the head of a banjo piled with scrambled eggs and then fried potatoes on top.

Kate gasped at the enormity of the portion.

He lifted the second cover. There sat a small green quilted pillow tied up like a lady's purse, and beside it lay two thick slabs of toast. Sam leaned in to inspect her meal. There were three little dishes full of something. One resembled strawberry jam. Then he noticed the cream and sugar and a teacup as thin as an eggshell.

Kate gasped.

Sam fumed. "Now why in blazes would they give you a teacup and saucer and no tea!"

"But there is tea!"

She lifted the little quilted doily to reveal a teapot secreted beneath. She raised the lid and steam rose from within. She leaned forward and inhaled. The smile that curled her lips did something to his insides.

"It's orange pekoe." She replaced the lid. "Oh, thank you, Sam. This is perfect."

"What are those?" he asked, pointing at the little bowls no bigger than shot glasses.

She indicated the first. "Butter, jam and orange marmalade."

"That enough?"

"Oh, most certainly." Kate drew off her gloves and set them beside her tray. Her palms still looked raw in places.

She pressed her index finger to the lid and lifted the pot, tipping it to send a graceful cascade of hot tea directly into her cup without losing a drop.

Sam took a seat as Kate added milk and one teaspoon of sugar. Somehow she stirred in the sugar without ever touching the edge of the fine cup. The thing would probably shatter if she even nicked it.

She clasped the tiny handle of the cup and smiled up at him. "This is lovely, Sam. Thank you."

"Jiminy, you didn't make this much fuss over the railroad stock I gave you."

She giggled and lifted the cup and saucer. He thought he'd wait to eat until he saw her take that first swallow. Something about seeing Kate enjoying herself was not to be missed.

He thought about the ring. Would she accept it? Had he convinced her that he was nothing like her first husband? If she'd accept him, he might have what he had lost, someone to love again. And he might have something he'd longed for—someone to love him.

"Sam, are you all right?" she asked.

He snapped out of his musings. "Yeah, why?"

She nodded toward the far end of the car and he heard what Kate obviously already had.

Some blamed idiot was knocking on the compartment door like a pileated woodpecker. Sam ignored it but the knocking grew more insistent.

Kate lowered her cup. Sam stood and threw his napkin to the seat of his chair.

"Excuse me," he said, and then muttered, "I have to crack open someone's skull."

Sam crossed the compartment in five angry strides and yanked open the door. Cole stood on the stairs with one fine snakeskin boot on the top of the platform. Something in his expression brought Sam to instant alert.

"What's happened?"

Sam held up a single folded sheet of paper. "You better read this. It came by courier a few minutes ago. It's from Crawford."

Sam had a strong premonition of disaster. He stepped out of the car and stood on the stairs. Cole handed over the note and retreated down the stairs. Sam looked at Cole once more for reassurance and instead saw a tight, guarded expression. His apprehension doubled.

"To hell with this," he said, and flipped open the page.

Mr. Ellis,

Please locate Mr. Pickett immediately and tell him that Kate Wells is implicated in the robbery that occurred on the eighteenth day of April of this year. It appears likely that she is in the employment of Mr. Robert Donahue. She is armed and all precautions should be taken.

I have possession of a gold necklace purchased by Mr. Pickett. It was found in the custody of Miss Barbara Burns, the co-conspirator who lured Mr. Pickett into the alley on the above date. Miss Burns alleges that Mrs. Wells gave the necklace to her for her part in the ruse perpetrated on Mr. Pickett.

Your servant,
Mr. Allen Crawford
Pinkerton Detective Agency
Sacramento Office

The page fluttered from Sam's hand to land in the dirt at Cole's feet.

Sam stood on the steps of the railcar, still as stone as his heart fell to dust. Inside his chest a great emptiness grew, tunneling like a mine shaft, vacant, hollow, cold.

"Sam, I…" Cole's words fell off.

What did you say to a man who had been played the fool?

"I wanted to marry her," whispered Sam, realizing he still wanted to. "My God, ain't I the prize-winning rube at the fair?"

He'd considered this possibility, even asked her point-blank if she'd been involved. But her astonishment and then outrage had been enough to convince him.

Sam clamped his mouth shut as he considered this final abandonment, the abandonment of his trust. Kate had confirmed what he had always feared. He was not worthy of love. His mother hadn't thought so, nor had his brother. They had tossed him away like so much garbage and now Kate had done the same.

He turned away from his friend in a vain effort to compose himself. What did a man do after his guts had been kicked out?

Sam slipped his hands into his pockets. His fingers touched the lid of the leather box. Sam dragged the thing from his trousers and threw it with all his might. It bounced off the sided of the railcar and came to rest near Cole's feet.

Cole stared at the dusty box. "What was that?"

My future, he thought. "Just another mistake."

He headed back up the steps. His legs now seemed cast of lead and his arms hung heavy at his sides.

"Remember she's got a gun," said Cole.

Sam stared at his friend. "Kinda pointless shooting a man who she's already stabbed in the back."

Sam trudged up the stairs as anxious to reach his destination as a condemned man. But he couldn't turn back until this whole charade was finished.

Of course he couldn't marry her. He couldn't marry anyone. No one wanted him or needed him. Nothing had changed except that for a few days he had forgotten that. But he was still the man he had always been, solitary, raw and aching.

He entered the car and found Kate still sitting properly before her untouched breakfast. Her smile faded as she took him in.

"Bad news?" she asked.

"Very bad." He made it to the chair and then clung to the back, squeezing the padding as if he meant to choke the life from it. "They caught the woman. The decoy from the alley."

Kate wrinkled her brow.

She must know now that he had unmasked her, yet her face revealed nothing. The woman should be on the stage.

"But that's good news, isn't it?" she asked.

So she would deny it to the last, then.

Why did he still want her when there was nothing between them but lies?

"Sam?" She rose now, standing beside her place.

"She says you two were partners."

Her forehead stayed wrinkled a moment, as if she didn't already know. He had a moment's doubt as her eyes rounded in an expression of complete surprise.

"But that's a lie!"

"Is it, or is everything you've said since I met you been the lie?"

She took a step toward him.

"Where's the necklace, Kate?"

She faltered and then stopped. She didn't have it. Still, his stupid heart clung to hope.

"Get it," he said, finding his words sounded more like a plea than an order.

Her head drooped. "I can't, Sam."

"Because you gave it to your partner."

Kate stood in a surreal world. What was happening? Her hand moved to her throat, touching the place where the necklace should have been.

She had never seen Sam like this. His face was pale and his visage grim as death. The muscle at his jaw ticked and a blood vessel twisted across his forehead, pulsing like a dying snake.

"I gave it to my aunt to pay our bills," she whispered.

He pressed his hand across his eyes as if he could no longer bear to look at her. She took another step in his direction, but something about his rigid posture made her stop. He'd never struck her, but he looked so angry, so bereft, it frightened her.

His hand slid away and she saw that his expression had changed. It was his eyes she noticed first. The sorrow had left them. Now he looked at her with the cold stare of a stranger, as if she meant nothing to him.

"It's over," he said.

Her heart pounded painfully in her chest. No, he couldn't send her away, not now, not when…

"But I love you," she cried.

He turned toward the window. "Don't. There's no point now."

"I'm sorry about the necklace, Sam. But we had debts. You knew why I agreed to this. But all that's changed now. Please, Sam. You have to forgive me."

He whipped around so fast that she staggered back.

"No, I don't. All this time, I've been pouring my heart out and you've been using me."

"No."

"Well, I won't be your fool any longer. You're leaving today. When you get back to San Francisco, tell Donahue hello."

"Sam, no."

But he was walking away, leaving her, sending her off.

She wanted to sink to her knees and weep, but instead she snatched up her gloves and reticule and followed him. He was already down the stairs by the time she reached the compartment door.

Kate glanced about and saw that they had arrived at the rail's end. Chinese laborers carried baskets of earth and wooden ties along the track. Mule teams pulled wagons of gravel along the parallel road. Beyond, a wall of rock loomed and at the base, a neat arched tunnel led into the darkness.

She caught sight of Sam and ran after him. His friend saw her first and said something to him. Sam turned and glared at her.

"Rider!" called the Pinkerton standing on the ridge overlooking the track. "Coming fast!"

They moved to the rocky outcrop beside the newly blasted tunnel. The rider appeared a few moments later, running at a gallop on a lathered, winded horse.

Sam glanced at Cole. "That Crawford?"

Cole nodded.

Crawford charged up the gentle grade leading to the terminus of the rails, his head swiveling as he approached the workers. He slowed to a canter and stood in his stirrups until he spotted them.

His dismount was smooth. He spoke to Cole. "You've got trouble coming. We kicked a hornet's nest. I filed charges on your behalf and Donahue sent his men after you both. They'll be here anytime."

Kate acted on instinct, moving close to Sam's side. Crawford's eyes narrowed on her as he spoke to Cole.

"He get my note?"

Sam stepped away from Kate. "I got it."

Kate looked from Sam to Crawford and her confusion hardened to understanding. She lowered her chin. "You're the one who told these lies about me!"

Crawford ignored her. "They'll be here in a few minutes. Might want to secure her for now."

"Secure her?" screeched Kate. She lunged at Crawford and Sam grasped her about the waist.

He spoke to Cole. "I'm sending her down."

Kate struggled. "No, Sam. I want to stay."

He snorted.

"Just lock her in a shed," said Crawford.

Sam ignored him and Cole stepped before him. "Might need that engine."

Sam gripped Kate's arm as she struggled for release and still faced off with Cole. "I'm sending her down."

Cole raised his hand in surrender as he stepped aside.

Sam grabbed Kate's upper arm and pulled her to the closest car, the one used to carry freight to the building site. It was one of two remaining cars still coupled to the engine and could be ready to roll in only a few minutes.

She clutched the black velvet bag that hung by ribbons to her wrist. Sam recalled Cole's warning, and thought it might be less painful if he just shot him and got it over with. But she did not draw her weapon. Instead, she swept forward and clung to him.

"I want to stay with you. Please don't send me away."

He peeled her hands off his lapels. "Might just as well sleep with a rattlesnake in my blanket."

"Don't Sam. Don't believe him. It's a lie."

He stared at her. She had betrayed him and all he could think to do was to send her away from danger, away from the possibility of harm.

She began to cry.

"That trick might have worked once, but no longer. Stay on this train till you hit Sacramento."

"You might need me."

He glared coldly. "I won't."

She looked at him as if he had struck her. Sam grabbed her around the waist and hoisted her like luggage into the empty compartment. Then he waved to the engineer. "Take her back down, Paul. Don't stop till you hit the main terminal."

A moment later the whistle blew.

Kate looked for a moment as if she might leap from the car.

Sam stared up at her. "I never want to see you again."

She staggered backward. He grabbed the handle and pulled. The heavy door rolled along the track, shutting her into the car. The last thing he saw was wide-eyed astonishment on her perfect face.

Chapter Twenty-One

Sam watched the train roll away.

Cole frowned. "You ought to be sending her to jail."

"Don't press me."

Cole raised an eyebrow.

Sam glared. "What makes you so damned sure that Crawford is right and Kate is wrong?"

Cole watched the engine chug away, billowing black smoke. "Okay, partner. We'll get to the bottom of it. But now, you need to focus on what's coming at us."

Sam nodded and Cole grabbed a pry bar and jacked open a crate of dynamite. Sam retrieved a coil of fuse.

"How many?" Cole asked Crawford.

"I counted seven. Donahue is out of the shadows and stepping up his attack, taking it right to you. Once you are both dead, there'll be nobody to stand against him." He pointed at Cole. "Donahue figured you'd fold if he threatened your family." He pointed at Sam. "He knew you wouldn't back down. But you were supposed to have died in that alley."

"Would have if not for Kate," said Sam.

"She just was smart enough to turn that situation to her advantage."

"Disobeying Donahue?" said Sam. "That's just a way to get killed."

Crawford had no answer.

Sam narrowed his eyes. "How do you know Kate betrayed me?"

"Later," said Cole. "They're coming."

"Now," said Sam.

Crawford shrugged. "Because her partner had your property."

"How'd she get it?"

"Said Kate gave it to her."

Kate didn't have the necklace. But that wasn't enough to condemn her in his book. He wished she'd been straight with him, but the woman had plenty of cause to be hesitant about trusting men. Sam had a hunch. It tingled inside him with the same intensity as the time he'd followed the tracer vein right back into the mountain to find the mother lode. He thought of Kate's face when he'd accused her. Just like a tracer vein, she'd given him a sign. The disbelief and confusion had been plain, but he'd been too hurt to see it.

"Why should I believe her over Kate?"

Crawford shifted. "Listen, I'm trying to do the job you paid me for. Mrs. Wells's integrity is in serious question. I don't know which one of them to believe."

"Well, I do." Sam stared at the line of smoke spewing from the engine. He glanced at Cole. "I think I just made the worst mistake of my life."

"She's not in on this?" asked Cole.

He shook his head. "I'd bet my life on it."

Cole reached into his pocket and handed Sam back the red leather ring box. Sam closed his fist around it.

It was dark inside the freight car. Kate squinted until her eyes adjusted. Her efforts to open the sliding door failed. She turned to the other side and noticed a beam of sunlight shining through a crack in the door on the opposite side of the car. The whistle gave a shriek and the cars lurched, throwing Kate to the floor.

She lay for a moment on the dirt planks, pressed down by despair.

He didn't believe her, but he had ignored that man's suggestion to lock her in the shed and he had ignored his best friend's observation that they might need the engine. Why would he do that?

Because he promised to protect you.

Kate gasped at the implication. He needed to send her *away* to protect her. She sat up.

"He's in danger."

She leaped to her feet. She had to get out. She had to get to Sam. Oh, God, what if something happened to him? What if those outlaws killed him?

Her blood turned icy as spring runoff.

"No, no. Sam!" She beat her fists against the door. "Let me out! Please, sweet Lord, let me out."

She glanced frantically about. Sunlight blinded her. She turned to see a crack of daylight and dashed to the opposite side of the car. She clutched the handle of the unlocked door and threw all her weight against it, pulling with all her might. It didn't budge. She screamed out her frustration. The train lurched and then began to roll. Panic bubbled up in her throat. She braced her back on the door and used both hands and one foot to push against the adjoining wall. The door rolled slowly aside, leaving an opening of just ten inches.

She thought of the gunmen and Sam as she gripped the side of the compartment and stared down at the rail ties, blurring beneath her feet. Suddenly, she understood her terror and her desperation to get to him. She couldn't lose him because, because…

She loved him. Finally, she had found a man she could trust, a man she could adore, and she would be damned if she'd let some outlaw take him from her.

The world beyond her car flew by at dizzying speed. Her breath caught.

Do you love him or not?

Kate held her breath and leaped.

She skidded on the gravel, tumbling down the incline. Her reticule thumped against the ground and then her leg with such force she feared her derringer might go off.

Behind her came the whooshing sound of gravel skittering. Kate's roll ended in an undignified slide on her bottom. She clawed like a madwoman at the loose shale and gravel, finally bringing herself to a stop.

Kate groaned as she crawled to her feet. She twisted to examine her posterior.

"Drat." The velvet and satin had torn from the waistband, leaving a gaping hole in her skirts that revealed her ravaged petticoats. She patted her behind. "Good padding, that."

Kate next discovered she had ruined another pair of

gloves, but they were, at least, intact and had protected her hands from further harm. Not so for her left elbow, which she had skinned. She smoothed her hair and recalled she hadn't had time to put on her hat. She brushed off her hind quarters, sending dust everywhere. Then she lifted her right arm and gave a startled cry.

"My bag!"

She searched the area and found it near the top of the incline. Her reticule had torn and she spent several minutes searching for her derringer, finding it, at last, glinting in the sun. She was forced to tuck the gun into the waistband of her skirt.

She glanced about. The train was out of sight, but the gray smoke rose above the pine trees as the engine chugged along, picking up speed on the down grade.

What should she do now?

Her question was answered a moment later with the explosion that shook the earth. This time, she recognized the sound of dynamite. She turned in time to see shattered timber flying skyward above the pines. An instant later there came the shriek of metal on metal and a crash that shook the earth. She could think of only one thing that could cause such tremor.

Kate scrambled up the incline toward the tracks.

Sam turned toward the explosion and then covered his ears at the deafening screech of the brakes seizing the twin rails. The thundering boom told him the engineer had failed to stop the engine in time.

Sam stared in horror.

"They blew the tracks," Cole said.

Sam stared in shock at the debris rising into the air. His stomach dropped as a plume of gray smoke continued to billow into the sky.

"Kate," he whispered.

She was on the train, he had forced her aboard.

Sam started running. Something tangled around his ankles and he fell facefirst into the road. He glanced back to find Cole lying on his legs. Sam lifted a boot to kick him off.

"Wait." He pointed. "Horses, rifles."

Crawford was already back in the saddle of his spent horse as Cole and Sam ran down the short incline to the corral where the horses were saddled.

They swung up in unison.

Sam spurred the mount, leaning low across the horse's neck.

Behind them, men shouted, but he ignored them. He couldn't think past reaching that train and getting to her.

Kate crested the tracks and stood on the wide tie just in time to see Sam tearing down the road on horseback with Cole close behind. They were already fifty yards past her and riding at a full gallop.

"Sam! I'm here! I'm safe!"

They did not pause.

Was he charging to her rescue or in pursuit of the perpetrators? It didn't matter. Sam was riding toward danger.

Kate lifted her dragging skirts in one hand and her derringer in the other and stormed down the tracks like an infantry soldier.

* * *

Cole and Sam knew better than to ride straight down the tracks, so they had left their horses and come at the wreck from the high ground, halfway up the ridge on the right of the rails.

Sam scanned the mayhem before him. The engine had jumped the tracks at the breach and now lay on its side, spewing steam. The coal car had disgorged its contents down the graded embankment and also lay on its side still tethered to the engine. Beyond that, the two crushed freight cars had splintered against the cliff side like empty packing crates thrown from a wagon.

Sam searched the wreckage for a glimpse of black velvet and found none. He was just about to charge down the track when his partner grasped his arm.

Cole pointed.

Men crept from cover, rifles ready as they inched toward the train.

"They think we're aboard," said Cole.

"Kate."

"You'll do her no good leaking blood."

Sam clenched his jaw. It was the first time since the mountain that they had disagreed.

"I'm for charging down there, guns blazing."

"How about we keep to cover until we know where they all are?"

Crawford crept along to join them, having secured their horses down the tracks a piece. Crawford drew up beside Cole and stared down at the three men. "Where are the others?"

Cole's jaw was granite. His eyes narrowed. "Hanging back, I'd imagine."

Sam lifted his rifle and took aim. Cole followed his example. Crawford, unfortunately had only a pistol and he wisely moved a few yards away and took cover.

"I got left," said Sam, his voice low and deadly.

"Right," replied Cole.

"On three, then. One, two." There was no need to say *three* as both shots exploded from the barrels and two men dropped. The third started running as Crawford fired and missed. Cole and Sam cocked their rifles and took aim. The gunman dove and made it behind the engine as the shots zinged past him.

"Damn it!" cursed Cole.

"Change location," said Crawford, holding his revolver as he headed up the embankment.

Cole and Sam crept between the boulders, keeping an eye out for the remaining men. They didn't have long to wait.

Kate froze at the sound of gunfire, squatting low on the tracks, then inched over the outer rail and scrambled down the embankment toward the woods. She reached the trees and discovered a narrow animal trail running parallel to the tracks. She lifted her dragging skirt and hurried along, her steps faltering when she glimpsed the wreckage through the forest.

What should she do? She wanted to help Sam, but did not want to distract him. She had only her tiny pistol with a range of just a dozen feet.

She crept along the trail, unsure who was shooting

and where they might be. She drew even with the derailment. Her eyes widened as she took in the destruction. One look at the two freight cars told them she would not have survived.

Shots cracked from an outcrop of rock above the train and return fire popped from close by. She squatted down, scanning until she located two men, hunkered behind the coal car waiting for the men on the ridge to quit firing. A little farther down she saw someone crawling from the engine. Blood covered the top of his head and one side of his face. He paused to drag another, unconscious man from the compartment. The engineers, she realized, had somehow survived the catastrophe.

Her peripheral vision caught movement. A man stood in the trees not twenty feet to her left. He pressed his chest to a thick trunk as he stared at the ridge. He drew his pistol and took aim, but then changed his mind and lowered his weapon.

Kate crept closer but stopped, lest he notice her. She hid in a grove of pines just off the tail. From here she saw the two by the coal car glance back at the trees. Kate crouched, afraid they had spotted her, until she realized that they looked to the man by the tree.

He held his fists side by side and then slowly separated them. The two men nodded. Did he want them to separate?

She glanced up and spotted Cole and Sam moving in opposite directions, just as the man before her had indicated. He was revealing their positions.

Kate spotted three men creeping down the ridge

toward Sam. She lifted a hand to her mouth to shout a warning. But before the words left her lips someone yelled from the top of the ridge. Three men sat on horseback, rifles raised. She recognized them, the men who had guarded Sam since he left Sacramento. The Pinkertons had arrived.

"Pickett! Behind you."

Sam whirled and fired, hitting the man on the left. The man screamed and clutched his face, falling backward and out of sight. The other men spun and began a rapid exchange with the Pinkertons above them, then dove behind a boulder. The Pinkertons retreated to cover, but Sam used the distraction to move to another spot, disappearing from her sight.

He popped up from behind a rock a moment later and shot one of the men above him in the chest. The man fell from the ridge, his body flailing until he collided with the rocks beside Cole.

The final man fired at Sam as he vanished again. Kate gasped, pressing her hand over her mouth to keep from screaming. Cole was standing now, firing at the remaining man, his bullets pinging off the rocks, pulverizing the stone into little puffs of dust.

Kate heard the shots nearby and saw Cole spin, clutching his shoulder, and then disappear behind the rocks. The two by the coal car had crept from cover and continued to fire even though their target had vanished.

Kate's breathing stopped. They had hit him. Hadn't they?

Above them, the Pinkertons now sent a heavy volley

of bullets down at the men on the tracks. Kate pressed her face into the crook of her arm and ducked behind a tree trunk as bullets zipped past her, shaking the leaves of the bushes.

Someone screamed. Kate peered out to see one of the men at the back of the coal car fall backward, his arms spread wide upon the ground as if he were surrendering. He thudded hard to the ground and then lay still. His partner crept toward him, squatted beside him for an instant and then resumed his position.

Kate stared up at the ridge. Cole was climbing higher as Sam and the detective pinned down the man above them with a flurry of shots. Cole drew even and, as the man swung his rifle toward him, he dropped the man with a single shot.

Sam was now charging down the steep incline, scrambling along until he hit the flat just before the engine.

"Kate!" he called.

The last outlaw took air at Sam. Kate lifted her derringer, knowing she was too far away for an accurate shot.

Chapter Twenty-Two

Kate fingered the trigger as a hail of bullets came from above her on the ridge. The Pinkerton's gunfire sent the man into retreat.

Sam continued running down the embankment, making no effort to seek cover as he made for the demolished freight car where she should have been riding. The Pinkertons on the ridge sent a barrage of shots at the remaining shooter, who was now sitting huddled in a ball with his back pressed to the coal car. He clutched his rifle between his hands as if aiming at the sky. He looked as if he were praying. At last he glanced back at the man still hidden in the woods. When the shooter on the tracks made a move to run toward him, he raised his pistol and aimed at his own man.

Sam had reached the other side of the coal car when his partner shouted.

The shooter by the coal car ran along the tracks toward the engine, passing the two injured men as bullets whizzed by him. Despite the Pinkertons' best efforts, he made it off the track and down the embankment below the tracks.

"After him, boys," called someone from the ridge.

"That's seven," shouted the detective.

Sam was already running for the debris. "I gotta find her."

Cole reached the level ground, keeping his rifle gripped in a bloody hand. He'd been hit.

Above him, the detectives picked their way carefully down the incline.

Kate noted the movement to her left and turned to see the final man, the other observer, raise his pistol. Kate aimed her derringer at him.

"Pickett," called the engineer. "Dietz is hurt."

Sam glanced toward the call, but then turned back to the wreckage.

"I got it," called Cole.

Cole disappeared from Kate's view and the man edged forward, paralleling Sam's path, coming closer to Kate.

She looked at the engineer for help, but he was removing his jacket, placing it under the head of his fallen partner. Sam crossed the tracks to check a small section of the car that had not splintered into a thousand pieces. He now stood only fifteen feet from her, but she kept her focus on the gunman as he stepped out of the cover of trees. He drew even with her and she cocked her two-shot pistol, closed one eye and took careful aim at the center of his chest.

He raised his revolver at Sam and Kate pulled the trigger.

He spun, his mouth drawn in a wide O of shock as he stared at her. His left hand came up and pressed against his chest, high up by his collarbone, as a red rose of blood spread across his white shirt. Then he lifted his revolver, pointing it at Kate. She fired her second shot at the same time she heard a rifle report. Her bullet missed. Sam's didn't.

Sam rose from one knee as the gunman dropped to his and then pitched forward to the earth.

Cole charged up the tracks, his rifle aimed at the fallen man. He checked around. "That all?"

Kate nodded. "I think so."

Sam ran to Kate. She dropped her pistol and threw herself into his arms. He absorbed the force of her charge and wrapped her in a warm embrace. They both spoke at once.

"I thought I'd lost you," he said.

"He was going to kill you," she said.

She ran her fingers through his hair, knocking off his hat.

Sam kissed her hard, the force revealing his fear and joy all at once. He drew back to look at her. "I can't believe you survived that."

She stared at the dead man, sprawled on the ground. "Me, neither."

Cole glanced at Sam. "Either of you hurt?"

They stared at each other and said "no" in unison.

"Got me, though. If anyone is interested." Cole thrust the index finger of his left hand into a tear in his jacket.

Kate remembered how he'd clasped his shoulder during the shoot-out.

"How bad?" asked Sam. He handed his rifle to Kate and tugged off his friend's coat.

Cole's white shirt was soaked with blood from just below the shoulder. He grabbed Cole's shirt and tore the sleeve open. The injury seemed more a long bloody gash than a hole.

"Nicked you," said Sam.

Cole twisted his arm for a better look. "Burns like a mother…" He glanced at Kate and closed his mouth.

"Bleeding's slowing down," said Sam. He took the two halves of the ragged sleeve and wrapped them around Cole's arm and tied them in a knot. "That'll do for now."

Cole tentatively prodded the covered wound with his fingers and winced. He glanced at Sam and then Kate. "Guess I'll see to Cohen and Dietz."

Kate could see that the detective had collected the three horses and was making his way along the track to the engineer as the two Pinkertons peeled down the tracks on horseback after the escaping man. The others fanned out, checking each dead man.

One man hurried toward them. "Mr. Ellis? You all right?"

Cole waved them down. "We got men hurt down here." He looked back at Kate and scowled. "Yet she has not one scratch. I wonder why?"

Cole turned and marched away.

Kate did not like that man.

Sam gripped her shoulders, scanning her from head to toe. "How? How did you survive that crash?"

She glanced away, wondering what he'd do if he discovered the truth.

"Kate?" Sam's voice grew low and dangerous. "You did that same thing when I asked about the necklace—looking at your toes as if they could talk. Answer me. How did you..."

She stared up at him and watched his eyes go round. "Did you jump off a moving train?"

She lowered her head. "It was barely moving."

"Sweet mother of us all!"

"It seemed the only way to help you."

"You could have been killed," bellowed Sam.

She thrust her fists into her hips, standing up for herself this time. "And you nearly were."

"You have to do what I tell you."

"Do you really think I would have been better off on that!" She nodded at the wreckage.

Sam went pale, but he rallied.

"That's not the point!"

"No? Well, if you want perfect obedience, perhaps you should have bought a hound instead of a woman."

He smiled.

That only made her madder. "Why are you smirking?"

"'Cause you're standing up to me instead of cowering. You aren't afraid of me anymore?"

Her heart squeezed tight and all the fight drained out of her. He was right. She was frightened, shaken and near tears, but this was a different kind of fear.

He cradled her face in his two broad hands. "I'm glad." His expression grew serious. "Kate? I don't want a trained hound."

She smiled. "No?"

His smile broadened. "I just want you safe."

Kate needed to tell him everything. She clutched his shirt and stared up at him.

"Sam, I didn't have anything to do with that other woman. I'm not her partner. And I don't have the necklace because I gave it to my aunt. I told her to sell it to settle our debts."

His eyes widened. "I knew it!"

"You did?"

"Not that you sold it, but that you didn't betray me."

"But Sam, how could you have known that?"

He smiled down at her. "I just had a hunch."

Kate wrinkled her brow in confusion. "A hunch?"

He rested his hands over hers. His smile faded as he gazed down at her. "Kate, why didn't you just ask me for the money? I'd have given it to you."

She felt her throat constricting. Of course he would have, because he was generous and kind and dear. He wouldn't try to manipulate her as Luke had done. She was ashamed of herself for not giving him the benefit of the doubt.

"Sam, Luke never gave me any money."

"What do you mean?"

"He didn't trust me. I thought you might be like-minded. I'm sorry."

"What'd he think you'd do with it—the money, I mean?"

"He correctly assumed that I would use it to run."

Sam's eyes widened again. "I'll be damned."

He dragged her into his arms and held her so tight she forgot to breathe.

"Sam? I have something else to tell you."

He eased up on his grip. Now the constriction in her chest was caused by her uncertainty. Was it a bad thing, for a mistress to fall in love with her employer? Bad for her, perhaps, because it gave him more power over her. But it wouldn't stop him from wanting her, would it?

He set her at arm's length to study her. "Kate? What is it? You've gone pale."

"I'm scared again. I've never felt like this before." In fact she felt more dizzy now than when she was preparing to jump from the moving train.

"Kate, we got them all. There's no danger now."

But she disagreed. It was the most dangerous thing she had ever done, because she was about to give her heart. Even Luke, with all his trickery and charm, had failed to win that.

"Sam, do you know why I jumped off that train?"

"To watch my hair turn gray?"

She didn't smile and his smile vanished, as well. Now he braced, waiting for her to speak. She closed her eyes and cast out a silent prayer that he would not reject her when he heard. Then she rested her open hands upon his wide, warm chest and drew a breath.

"I've fallen in love with you, Sam."

His eyes widened and the he scowled. "Well, hell, woman. You make it sound like you caught some disease."

"It scares me, is all."

He grinned at her now, looking a little misty and very pleased with himself. "Really? You love me?"

She nodded.

"I'll be damned."

A small part of her had secretly hoped that he might

confess his love for her, as well. It was the sort of romantic notion that had caused her to accept everything Luke had told her at face value.

Sam continued to grin and she began to wish she had not told him.

A young Pinkerton interrupted them. "Mr. Pickett, we found no survivors among your attackers. My boys are after the one that escaped."

Sam released her to face the man. "My men?"

"Both alive, sir." He stooped to pick up something silver and cradled the derringer in his palm. "Yours, miss?"

She nodded and reclaimed the pistol. Kate glanced at the thing a moment. This little bit of metal and powder had saved Sam's life.

Best gift Luke ever gave me, she thought, and tucked the derringer into the waistband of her skirt.

Sam spoke to the guard. "Get a wagon up here to carry the bodies back to camp. Then send a rider down to Sacramento. We're going to need another engine and the biggest winch system we can find."

"Yes, sir." The man headed off.

Sam looped an arm around Kate's waist, drawing her closer.

"Jumped, huh?" He turned her around, taking in her drooping skirts and muddy petticoats. "You sure are hard on the duds I bought you. Been through two of them in as many days. Might be better to dress you in dungarees."

"You might be better to get me a holster for this as I seem to be forced into the position of bodyguard."

He squeezed her shoulder and she looked up at him,

expecting to see the teasing smirk. Instead, she found him looking thoughtful and serious.

"Thank you for not dying, Kate."

"You're welcome."

"Did you like the necklace?" He was changing the subject.

"It was beautiful." And cold and impersonal. "But my family's needs come before mine. And besides…" She couldn't tell him what she'd thought at the time. It would only hurt him.

"What?"

"It's nothing."

"Kate, tell me what you're thinking so I can understand."

She drew a breath and faced him. He had asked for the truth and she would oblige him.

"Luke gave me jewelry. A lot of it. Lovely, glittering things that he made me wear when he showed me off to the men he swindled. He used me as bait, do you understand? An enticement, like those little silver fishing lures that shine and flash in the water so the big fish will come and take a bite." She rested a dirty gloved hand on his wrist. "Can you understand? You came along and bought me that lovely necklace and all new clothing and then told me you wanted me at Dutch Flats when you spoke to the miners. Do you remember?"

"Just like he did." He met her gaze and she thought she saw regret in his eyes. "You make me feel ashamed of wanting to show you off."

"No, it's different with you. You don't treat me like

a decoy. You gave me that railroad stock, a gift from your heart, and you brought me that tea this morning."

"Which you never got to drink."

She flushed, recalling their separation.

"I think I understand," he said. "But Kate, you'd be an asset to any man."

She lifted her chin so she could meet his eyes. Did he think so? Did he see her as more than a fair face wrapped up in satin and glittering jewels? She needed to know.

"Sam? I want to ask you something, as well." She drew in as much air as her corset would allow. "Why did you put me on that train and why did you run down that hill to try to find me?"

He stared down at her. "Don't you know?"

Her heart jumped as hope beat inside her like a flock of sparrows taking flight.

"Why, Sam?"

"Because I've fallen in love with you, Kate."

She gasped as Sam stared at her with cautious eyes. Then she threw herself against him again, pressing tight to his warm chest as she kissed him full on the lips.

He moved his hand through her hair, sending pins flying as she kissed him with everything she had.

When they drew apart, they were both breathless.

"You've been through hell since I met you. But I plan to make it up to you, if you'll let me. I swear I'm not like him. I'll never raise a hand to you. That's a promise."

"I know that now, Sam."

"And I don't mind you thinking for yourself most times." He eyed the splintered remains of the freight car, before directing his attention back at her. "And I won't treat you like some China doll, though I'd like to spoil you a little, Kate. I want you to have pretty things."

"I'll be happy to accept them."

"And not hock them?"

She laughed. "Not if I can also keep my family safe and well cared for."

"I can do that."

Now she found her voice failed her. No man had ever seen fit to help her family.

"Maybe we can get Phoebe a tutor or something."

The tears were streaming down her face an instant later. Sam's eyes rounded in alarm.

"Just an idea, Kate. We don't have to get a tutor."

"Oh, Sam." She threw her arms around him. "How I love you."

He patted her back until the tears slowed and she drew away.

"So that was a good idea?" he asked, his voice uncertain.

She laughed and nodded. "I confuse you, don't I?"

"That's a fact." Sam's smile was dazzling. "So you promise? No more hocking jewelry?"

She placed a hand over her heart. "I swear."

Sam reached into his pocket and drew out a small, dusty, red leather box.

Sam stared down at his closed fist. She rested a hand on his forearm.

"Sam?"

He smiled, but his face showed strain.

"What's wrong?" she asked.

"Just more afraid now than I was the last time I was up on this mountain."

She gripped his arm. "I don't understand."

"You will," he promised, and sank to one knee before her.

Kate could think of only one reason a man would assume such a position and the realization hit her so hard her heart began a painful flutter.

Sam clasped her hand.

"Kate, I told you already I love you. And I don't think of you as…what'd you call it? A lure? I want you at my side as a partner, because you're smart and brave and, well, you're beautiful, too, of course."

"Oh, Sam."

"Let me get it out, now." He cleared his throat. "You had a man who didn't deserve you once. But if you let me, I'll try so hard to deserve you. I swear I'm nothing like him. And it's true that I don't know much about how to raise a family, but I'm a quick study and if you're willing, I'd like to have one, a family, I mean."

Her voice was breathless now, as if she'd just run down the tracks. "Sam, are you asking me to be your wife?"

He nodded glumly. "I know you said you'd never marry again. But I want to change your mind. I want you to marry me, Kate."

He flipped open the ring box to reveal a dazzling, sparkling rainbow of light. He pinched the ring between his thumb and forefinger and offered it to her.

She stared at him, feeling both humbled and honored. This wonderful man wanted her as his wife.

"Say yes, Kate."

She extended her bare hand and he slipped the ring into place. Kate stared a minute at the diamond ring and then smiled at Sam.

"Yes," she said.

Sam shot to his feet and dragged her off hers. He spun her around in a circle and then set her gently back to earth, but she swore her feet still did not touch the ground.

From down the track came the sound of several men cheering.

The following morning, Cole sat with Kate in the ornate parlor car as Sam finished supervising the repair of the track.

A new engine had arrived from Sacramento. The dead had been placed on board and the wounded engineer and his assistant were resting in the bunkhouse railcar.

Outside the window, two Pinkertons led the shackled surviving shooter toward the train. He had been captured, uninjured and they were taking him to the city to be charged.

Cole said, "He's our proof that Donahue's behind this. Glad they didn't kill him."

The Pinkertons marched past them with their prisoner and out of sight. Kate turned to Cole to find him studying her.

"It's rude to stare, Mr. Ellis."

He grinned. "I'm still trying to get my mind around Sam finding a wife."

"And you disapprove of his choice." There were many reasons he could. She had been married before and to a notorious man. She had been Sam's mistress.

She would not come to this marriage a virgin, of course. She would be less than an ideal choice in the minds of many, including, unfortunately, Sam's very best friend. And if all that were not reason enough to object, her loyalty had been called into question. Sam no longer believed she had betrayed him and that should have been enough, but she would have liked the blessing of her fiancé's best friend and partner.

It saddened her, for she had great respect for Cole and the tenacity with which he guarded Sam.

"Why would you think that?" he asked.

Now he had her off balance. "It's plain that you are less than jubilant about his choice."

"I told him he should throw you in jail."

Kate grimaced.

"And I'm sorry about that," he said. "I was trying to protect him. But I was wrong about you. Point being, Sam didn't listen to a word I said and that's a first. He believed *you,* even when Crawford told him you were guilty and I told him to lock you up. It's how I know he loves you."

She stared at him, completely speechless.

Cole gave a roguish smile. "We've had a bad start. You think we can be friends?"

"I'm sure of it."

Kate extended her properly gloved hand to him and he took if briefly. Cole glanced out the window.

"Here comes Sam. I'm going."

"Thank you for sitting with me."

Cole nodded, grabbed his hat and headed out the door. A moment later, Cole appeared outside the car and stopped before Sam. Cole patted Sam on the back and Sam grinned, glancing at Kate. She waved.

The men separated and Sam entered the car. She stood and he kissed her on the cheek, holding her hand tenderly.

"I left in such a hurry this morning, I never asked how you slept." His devilish smile told her that he was recalling the night they had spent wrapped in the sheets and each other's arms.

She feigned an air of indifference. "Oh, I slept quite soundly. It must be the mountain air."

She said this without so much as the hint of a smile, but Sam knew she was teasing and laughed. She smiled, pleased that he understood her dry humor.

"Kate, I wanted to say something to you about yesterday. I'm sorry I sent you away. Sorry I believed that blasted detective and his blather over you. I won't ever do that again."

She smiled, but it slipped away. Something still confused her. She understood why he would believe what was written in that message. What she couldn't understand was why he didn't believe it.

"What changed your mind?" she asked.

"I just stopped listening to what others said and started listening to my heart. I trust you, Kate. I knew you wouldn't do something like that. I was just confused for a little while."

She felt the tears brimming as she rested her head on his shoulder. His trust was the most precious of all the gifts he had given her.

Sam hugged her and then pulled her down beside him on the couch.

"I got something for you. Don't worry, it's not jewelry."

"Oh, Sam, you don't need to keep giving me gifts."

"I made it."

That got her curious. He held out his closed fist, palm down. She offered her palm and he dropped something light into it.

She drew it in. There, floating on the white surface of her gloved palm, was a perfectly carved wooden swan. Its graceful neck was arched and he had added two tiny black stones for the bead-black eyes.

"Oh, Sam!"

"I carved it from a dead limb of that tree you won't let me cut down."

"When did you have time to do this?"

"That day I went up to speak to the cartographer. Had to wait around a bit and, well, it's just a small thing."

She held it pressed tight to her heart. "I love it."

He grinned. "Do you? That's what you looked like to me at first, sitting in that tree after the flood—a swan."

Kate placed it before her on the table to admire it. "You have a talent. You should carve children's toys."

Their eyes met. Was he wondering if he'd have an opportunity to carve them for their children? She hoped so.

A knock came at the door. Sam did not swear, but instead hurried to answer it.

"I got you something else," he said to her and opened the door.

"Oh, no Sam. You've given me too much already."

"But you'll like this. I know it." He waved for someone to enter.

In stepped a Chinese man carrying a bamboo tray.

Upon it sat two very small teapots, two very small cups, sugar, cream and a little plate of something she did not recognize.

"This here is Wang. He's got some kind of mucketymuck of tea. Did ceremonies just for drinking tea back in Guangdong. Said they don't use cream, but he's making an exception."

"Oh, Sam!" She clasped her hands together in delight.

Sam pointed out the window. "See that man with the rifle standing there? He's got orders to shoot anyone who tries to interrupt us and this train will not roll until you have finished the pot."

Kate laughed as she took her seat.

Sam plopped next to her on the couch. "See these things?" He pointed at the plate. "They're flowers made out of sugar. You just drop them in your teacup. And these here are some kind of rice cookie. Real crispy. They taste like almond. I hope you like them. Wang made them in the cook tent early this morning."

Wang ignored the armchair and knelt before them on the floor, then carefully arranged all the various accessories. He used a small clean towel to wipe the lip of the empty ceramic. Then he flawlessly poured the piping hot water into each cup and immediately discarded the water, while warming the pottery. Finally, he poured the tea.

She sat forward in anticipation as he clasped a cup between both hands, bowed his head and offered the steaming hot tea to Kate.

Epilogue

Phoebe was now a young lady of thirteen, but Kate could tell it took great effort for her sister to keep from bouncing in her seat in excitement as the train neared the depot in Boston.

Sam had been true to his word, seeing Kate's family with love and devotion. He had even hired tutors from the east to school Phoebe. But he'd been reluctant to allow her to attend the Perkins School. It had taken both Phoebe and Kate nearly two years to convince him, since he had a horror of all institutions. Kate understood it. His early ears had certainly been difficult.

But they had finally arrived. Sam had business in Washington, convincing senators to back the necessary land grants needed to compete the railroad, and Phoebe was enrolled as a new student for the fall semester in the Perkins School for the Blind.

"Are you nervous, Phoebe?" asked Sam.

Kate shook her head, knowing that nothing she had said could convince him that this was a fine school where Phoebe would be well treated.

"Of course she's not nervous. We'll be just down the road on Pearl Street, so she can come home as often as she likes," said Kate, readjusting the wiggling bundle on her shoulder. Sam had insisted on buying a house right in the city so he could be sure Phoebe was happy.

Aunt Ella sat beside Phoebe, staring in wonder out the window of the private railroad car. "Look at the buildings! That one is five stories!"

Sam extended his arms toward Kate. "Let me take her."

"She just won't sit still," she said.

Sam grasped his eight-month-old daughter about the middle and lowered her between his legs, where she bounced and gurgled with delight, standing on her tiptoes. Sam secured her with both hands, allowing her to do what she could to keep upright. Abigail stretched out her tiny hands toward Phoebe.

"Oh, see? She wants to come to her aunt," said Sam.

Phoebe leaned forward and reached out in his direction. "Give me her hand."

But instead Sam released his hold on Abigail, keeping his palms just inches from her sides.

Abigail rocked back and forth for a moment, trying to find her balance, but this time she did not fall. Kate held her breath.

Abigail lifted a chubby leg and took her first step.

Ella gasped.

"What happened?" asked Phoebe.

Sam's voice was full of childlike wonder. "Did

you see that? Phoebe, put your arms out. She's walking to you."

Phoebe reached, opening her arms and cooing toward the baby she could not see. "Here I am, Abby. Come to Aunt Phoebe."

Abigail gurgled, lowering her chin in determination as she tottered across the gap between them on her toes. She reached Phoebe with a shriek of delight and Phoebe enfolded her in her arms.

"She did it!" cried Phoebe, scooping up her niece and bouncing her on one knee in celebration.

Sam turned to Kate, the wonder shining on her face. It was too much for Kate, who burst into tears.

Sam gathered his wife into his arms, kissing her forehead tenderly.

Phoebe turned toward her aunt. "Is Kate crying again?"

"Yes, again," said Ella.

Kate retrieved her handkerchief from her bag and dabbed her eyes. "I'm just happy."

Sam wrapped an arm about his wife. "The first time she did this, well, never mind the first time, the point is that it's hard to reconcile tears and happiness."

Phoebe giggled. "Haven't you ever heard of tears of joy?"

"I reckon. Just had limited experience with them."

Kate felt her heart constrict. Sam had not led a joyful life. But things were changing.

The train chugged along, the blasts of the whistle announcing their arrival. Kate looked out the window at the bustling city, so different from California. It was what she loved best about the journey eastward, seeing the landscape change. Here in New England, everything was a leafy, lush green.

The train rolled to a stop before the platform, where folks waited with craning necks for a glimpse of a loved one. She watched a lad running toward their private car clutching a telegraph.

Sam went to the door to meet the boy, accepting the envelope and tipping the carrier.

Kate tugged at her lace gloves as she waited for Sam to scan the contents of the message. Kate wondered if Crawford had returned from the South Seas, where he had pursued Donahue. The shipper had certainly led the Pinkerton on a merry chase. Kate had all but given up hope the man would every face justice. Sam had set the detective the task of running the former shipper to ground after he fled San Francisco ahead of the law.

Sam finished reading a moment later and his arm dropped limp at his side. His jaw opened, but nothing came out.

Kate was on her feet and hurrying to Sam. She grasped the telegram and read.

Donahue captured in Tahiti stop
Returned to San Francisco for trial stop
Pursuing second assignment stop
Brother located stop
Living in Mystic, Connecticut stop
Wishing to visit you with his wife, Mary
and sons, William and Samuel stop.
Please advise stop.
Cole Ellis

"Why Sam, this is wonderful! They've found him."

"Who?" asked Phoebe, now struggling to hold Abigail who wanted to be set down to try out her new steps. The baby had both hands over her head in an effort to slip out of her aunt's grip.

"Sam's brother. He lives here in the East and he wants to meet us."

Sam beamed as he hugged his wife. When she drew back, she saw tears forming in Sam's eyes.

"I have a family again," he whispered.

Phoebe lowered Abigail to the floor, keeping a firm grip on both her small hands. "What's wrong with Sam's voice?"

Kate withdrew her handkerchief and wiped Sam's eyes.

"I think Sam is just experiencing his first tears of joy."

* * * * *

Celebrate Harlequin's 60th anniversary
with Harlequin® Superromance®
and the DIAMOND LEGACY miniseries!

Follow the stories of four cousins as they
come to terms with the complications of love
and what it means to be a family. Discover
with them the sixty-year-old secret that rocks
not one but two families in...
A DAUGHTER'S TRUST by Tara Taylor Quinn.

Available in September 2009 from
Harlequin® Superromance®

RICK'S APPOINTMENT with his attorney early Wednesday morning went only moderately better than his meeting with social services the day before. The prognosis wasn't great—but at least his attorney was going to file a motion for DNA testing. Just so Rick could petition to see the child…his sister's baby. The sister he didn't know he had until it was too late.

The rest of what his attorney said had been downhill from there.

Cell phone in hand before he'd even reached his Nitro, Rick punched in the speed-dial number he'd programmed the day before.

Maybe foster parent Sue Bookman hadn't received his message. Or had lost his number. Maybe she didn't want to talk to him. At this point he didn't much care what she wanted.

"Hello?" She answered before the first ring was complete. And sounded breathless.

Young and breathless.

"Ms. Bookman?"

"Yes. This is Rick Kraynick, right?"

"Yes, ma'am."

"I recognized your number on caller ID," she said, her voice uneven, as though she was still engaged in whatever physical activity had her so breathless to begin with. "I'm sorry I didn't get back to you. I've been a little…distracted."

The words came in more disjointed spurts. Was she jogging?

"No problem," he said, when, in fact, he'd spent the better part of the night before watching his phone. And fretting. "Did I get you at a bad time?"

"No worse than usual," she said, adding, "Better than some. So, how can I help?"

God, if only this could be so easy. He'd ask. She'd help. And life could go well. At least for one little person in his family.

It would be a first.

"Mr. Kraynick?"

"Yes. Sorry. I was… Are you sure there isn't a better time to call?"

"I'm bouncing a baby, Mr. Kraynick. It's what I do."

"Is it Carrie?" he asked quickly, his pulse racing.

"How do you know Carrie?" She sounded defensive, which wouldn't do him any good.

"I'm her uncle," he explained, "her mother's— Christy's—older brother, and I know you have her."

"I can neither confirm nor deny your allegations, Mr. Kraynick. Please call social services." She rattled off the number.

"Wait!" he said, unable to hide his urgency. "Please," he said more calmly. "Just hear me out."

"How did you find me?"

"A friend of Christy's."

"I'm sorry I can't help you, Mr. Kraynick," she said softly. "This conversation is over."

"I grew up in foster care," he said, as though that gave him some special privilege. Some insider's edge.

"Then you know you shouldn't be calling me at all."

"Yes… But Carrie is my niece," he said. "I need to see her. To know that she's okay."

"You'll have to go through social services to arrange that."

"I'm sure you know it's not as easy as it sounds. I'm a single man with no real ties and I've no intention of petitioning for custody. They aren't real eager to give me the time of day. I never even knew Carrie's mother. For all intents and purposes, our mother didn't raise either one of us. All I have going for me is half a set of genes. My lawyer's on it, but it could be weeks—months—before this is sorted out. Carrie could be adopted by then. Which would be fine, great for her, but then I'd have lost my chance. I don't want to take her. I won't hurt her. I just have to see her."

"I'm sorry, Mr. Kraynick, but…"

* * * * *

*Find out if Rick Kraynick will ever have
a chance to meet his niece.
Look for A DAUGHTER'S TRUST
by Tara Taylor Quinn,
available in September 2009.*

**We'll be spotlighting a different series
every month throughout 2009
to celebrate our 60th anniversary.**

**Look for Harlequin® Superromance®
in September!**

*Celebrate with
The Diamond Legacy
miniseries!*

Follow the stories of four cousins as they come to terms
with the complications of love and what it means to
be a family. Discover with them the sixty-year-old secret
that rocks not one but two families.

A DAUGHTER'S TRUST by *Tara Taylor Quinn*
September

FOR THE LOVE OF FAMILY by *Kathleen O'Brien*
October

LIKE FATHER, LIKE SON by *Karina Bliss*
November

A MOTHER'S SECRET by *Janice Kay Johnson*
December

Available wherever books are sold.

You're invited to join our Tell Harlequin Reader Panel!

By joining our new reader panel you will:

- Receive Harlequin® books—they are FREE and yours to keep with no obligation to purchase anything!
- Participate in fun online surveys
- Exchange opinions and ideas with women just like you
- Have a say in our new book ideas and help us publish the best in women's fiction

In addition, you will have a chance to win great prizes and receive special gifts!
See Web site for details. Some conditions apply.
Space is limited.

To join, visit us at
www.TellHarlequin.com.

REQUEST YOUR FREE BOOKS!

 Harlequin® Historical
Historical Romantic Adventure!

2 FREE NOVELS PLUS 2 FREE GIFTS!

YES! Please send me 2 FREE Harlequin® Historical novels and my 2 FREE gifts (gifts are worth about $10). After receiving them, if I don't wish to receive any more books, I can return the shipping statement marked "cancel". If I don't cancel, I will receive 6 brand-new novels every month and be billed just $4.94 per book in the U.S. or $5.49 per book in Canada. That's a savings of 20% off the cover price! It's quite a bargain! Shipping and handling is just 50¢ per book.* I understand that accepting the 2 free books and gifts places me under no obligation to buy anything. I can always return a shipment and cancel at any time. Even if I never buy another book, the two free books and gifts are mine to keep forever.

246 HDN EYS3   349 HDN EYTF

Name	(PLEASE PRINT)	
Address		Apt. #
City	State/Prov.	Zip/Postal Code

Signature (if under 18, a parent or guardian must sign)

Mail to the **Harlequin Reader Service:**
IN U.S.A.: P.O. Box 1867, Buffalo, NY 14240-1867
IN CANADA: P.O. Box 609, Fort Erie, Ontario L2A 5X3

Not valid to current subscribers of Harlequin Historical books.

Want to try two free books from another line?
Call 1-800-873-8635 or visit www.morefreebooks.com.

* Terms and prices subject to change without notice. Prices do not include applicable taxes. Sales tax applicable in N.Y. Canadian residents will be charged applicable provincial taxes and GST. Offer not valid in Quebec. This offer is limited to one order per household. All orders subject to approval. Credit or debit balances in a customer's account(s) may be offset by any other outstanding balance owed by or to the customer. Please allow 4 to 6 weeks for delivery. Offer available while quantities last.

Your Privacy: Harlequin Books is committed to protecting your privacy. Our Privacy Policy is available online at www.eHarlequin.com or upon request from the Reader Service. From time to time we make our lists of customers available to reputable third parties who may have a product or service of interest to you. If you would prefer we not share your name and address, please check here. ☐

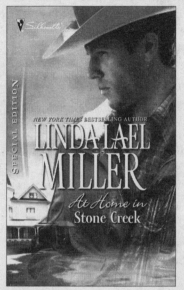

COMING NEXT MONTH FROM
HARLEQUIN®
HISTORICAL

Available August 25, 2009

- **THE PIRATICAL MISS RAVENHURST**
  by **Louise Allen**
  (Regency)
  Forced to flee Jamaica disguised as a boy, Clemence Ravenhurst falls
  straight into the clutches of one of the most dangerous pirates in the
  Caribbean! Nathan Stanier, disgraced undercover naval officer, protects
  her on their perilous journey. But who can protect his carefully guarded
  heart from her?
  The final installment of Louise Allen's Those Scandalous Ravenhursts
  miniseries!

- **THE DUKE'S CINDERELLA BRIDE**
  by **Carole Mortimer**
  (Regency)
  The Duke of Stourbridge thought Jane Smith a servant girl, so when
  Miss Jane is wrongly turned out of her home for inappropriate behavior
  after their encounter, the Duke takes her in as his ward. Jane knows she
  cannot fall for his devastating charm. Their marriage would be forbidden—
  especially if he were to discover her shameful secret....
  The first in Carole Mortimer's The Notorious St. Claires *miniseries*

- **TEXAS WEDDING FOR THEIR BABY'S SAKE**
  by **Kathryn Albright**
  (Western)
  Caroline Benet thought she'd never see soldier Brandon Dumont again—but
  the shocking discovery that she is carrying his child forces her to find
  him.... Darkly brooding Brandon feels his injuries hinder him from being
  the man Caroline deserves, so he will marry her in name only. It takes a
  threat on Caroline's life to make him see he could never let her or their
  unborn child out of his sight again....
  The Soldier and the Socialite

- **IN THE MASTER'S BED**
  by **Blythe Gifford**
  (Medieval)
  To live the life of independence she craves, Jane has to disguise herself as
  a young man! She will allow no one to take away her freedom. But she
  doesn't foresee her attraction to Duncan—who stirs unknown but delightful
  sensations in her highly receptive, very feminine body.
  He would teach her the art of sensuality!

HHCNMBPA0809